Books by William Mulvihill

Night of the Axe

William Mulvihill

BOSTON
Houghton Mifflin Company
1972

A SCORE OF CENTURIES had passed and the great tree still lived and grew, thicker and taller than any other on the eastern slope of the Sierra Nevada, deeply rooted in the rocky soil, between the desert and the high peaks above. No white man had ever seen it.

An eagle, soaring high above the tree that was its home and the center of its territory, saw again the snake-like column of men and animals moving slowly up the mountain, toward the tree, closer today than the day before.

The Tree

1

"My God," Webster Shaughnessey said.

Jamie Mecom glanced sideways at Webster, then saw, on the slope ahead, a tree which towered above all the rest, an evergreen so tall that it must be perched atop some abrupt rise, a hillock of its own.

"Look above it," Jamie said. "Some sort of hawk or eagle."

They looked up, shielding their eyes from the glare of the sun, and saw a dark blur hovering in the blue sky above.

Ten feet behind them, Jones, the Mountain Man, nodded to himself. The Mecom boy had good eyes. Shaughnessey, a city man, couldn't see goddamn unless you rubbed his nose in it, even with his pair of fool eyeglasses.

They were walking, resting their mounts, trudging up

the slope on legs used to level land. Webster Shaughnessey wondered how many more steps he could take before he quit and crawled back onto his winded horse; Jamie Mecom was seventeen, a farmboy from backwoods Missouri, and nothing seemed to tire him. Jones, damn him, old Jones was as strong as a horse and if he felt the urge he might just trot all the way over the mountain without waiting for the rest of the party. None of them had ever known anyone like Jones, a true Mountain Man, the last of a breed that had all but vanished with the beaver. They'd come upon him two days after their party had split off from the main group, a stooped and scrawny man, as brown as an Indian, walking north with only the greasy buckskins he wore and his rifle, the sole survivor, he'd said, of an ill-fated trapping expedition. When Mr. Benedict, their leader, told him that the party was headed for California, he'd shrugged and joined them. "Might as well point my needle that way as another," he'd explained.

"That's a *tree,*" Jamie said. "Lord almighty."

Webster Shaughnessey didn't answer. He steadied his horse and swung slowly up into the saddle, grunting with pleasure with the weight off his feet. He kicked the animal and moved ahead of the others.

Jamie Mecom hurried on, his eyes on the tree that seemed to be growing taller as they came closer, moving upward in the sky, higher and higher. Then he was on his horse, urging it forward, following Webster, forgetting that the animal was spent, forgetting that he was acting like a boy instead of a man of seventeen.

Webster halted on the open piece of level ground a

hundred yards from the base of the tree. He dismounted. Jamie did the same, sliding off his quivering animal. He turned, his face flushed, started to speak and then turned back, staring upward. The tree was fabulously tall and thick; gigantic, surrounded by others that although huge themselves, were, by comparison, slight and puny.

"Can't believe it," Jamie said. "Just can't believe it." He began to laugh, walking faster, then he was running, filled with an urge to seize the tree, hold it. And then Webster was beside him, running too, and they both suddenly knew they were in a childlike but desperate race to see who'd be the first to touch it.

Webster slipped on the needles and went down. Jamie reached the tree, digging his fingers into the shaggy bark, clutching it with outstretched arms, still laughing, gasping for breath. Webster got up and went to the tree, breaking off a piece of bark, staring upward. Then, still out of breath, he walked slowly around the great buttressing roots. On the far side there was an old fire scar which reached up forty or fifty feet, wide at the base, narrowing as it went up, the edges turned inward with new growth, a wound that the ancient tree had, long ago, suffered and survived.

He came back to Jamie who sat with his back against the tree, legs outstretched, examining one of the long pine cones that littered the ground. He slumped down, sweaty and still breathing deeply.

"We found ourselves some tree," Jamie said.

"We sure did — it's the grandest thing I've ever seen," Webster said. He put his head back and closed his eyes.

He was weary from the hours in the saddle and trudging up the slope on foot. It would be pleasant if there was time to sit here, rest, against the unbelievable tree, to fall asleep in the silence broken only by the singing of birds.

He opened his eyes. The Mountain Man was walking up the gentle slope, leading his horse.

"What'd you think of her?" Jamie shouted.

"Never seen one bigger."

"You mean that?" Jamie said. "You really mean that?"

"It's a fact, boy."

"I've heard about big trees," the boy said, "but I never figured the likes of this . . . *Damn!*"

Jones cleared his throat and spat. "I've seen big fellows but none to match this — there'll be water close by — seems like I smell it — monstrous thing like this needs plenty water."

He untied his pack roll and let it fall to the ground, then he bent down, unbuckled the cinch and pulled the saddle free from the horse, which tossed its head and trotted away.

Webster stared. "What's that for?"

"I'm stayin'," Jones said.

"We can't stay."

"They'll stop. Whole party. They'll stop, look around, make camp."

"Benedict told us to keep moving."

Jones walked toward them, wiping his hands on his greasy buckskin pants. He squatted down, smiling, brushed back his long stringy hair. "Move, if you're minded to. This hoss is sittin' loose."

Webster took out his gold watch. It wasn't much after noon. If they didn't move on, half the day would be wasted.

"It's just a little after noon," he said. "We can't stop. We picked Benedict to lead us and we oughta do what he says."

Jones sat down, then stretched out full length in front of them. He yawned noisily and folded his hands over his chest, closed his eyes.

"Seems like this Mista Benedict of yours wants too much from a man." He yawned again, a man no longer young, thin and scrawny but yet with a quality of ferocity; there was no doubt in Webster's mind that he'd killed men with his rifle, with his knife, with his gnarled, claw-like hands.

Webster stood up, brushed the bark dust and needles from his black coat. They'd leave Jones here. Let Benedict handle him.

"We better keep moving."

Jamie nodded. He wanted to stay by the tree and yet Webster was right. They had to get over the mountain. They couldn't lose any more time — even for the wonderful tree. He'd been proud when Mr. Benedict had asked him to scout ahead of the party with Jones and Webster. It showed he was trusted, a man.

"You'd both be smarter to rest your bones," Jones said, his eyes still closed. "Rest of them ain't likely to leave here, not when they see this tree — and I smell fresh water."

"Damn," Jamie said suddenly. "I hate to leave." He wanted to be here when the whole party arrived, his

7

brother Dallas and Naomi, especially Naomi. He wanted to watch her face when she first saw the tree.

"We've got to keep moving," Webster said. "Benedict won't stop. Tree or no tree, we've got no more time to fritter away."

"They'll stop," Jones said. "Then they'll want to stay put. Them people is still bone weary."

"He might be right," Jamie said. The party had rested for three days at the bottom of the mountain, beaten and exhausted from the desert, and if it hadn't been for Mr. Benedict they'd still be there. Mr. Benedict had argued with his brother Dallas and Jones and convinced the rest of the party that they must move on, start up the mountain before the snow came.

Webster felt the blood rise in his face.

"You coming or not?" he said too loudly.

The boy hesitated, started to rise, then saw the faint smile on Jones's face.

"I'll stay here," he said suddenly. Damn Webster. He was smart as hell, been to a university but Jones was a Mountain Man. Someday he was going to be like Jones, a free man, a true man.

Webster walked away. His horse and Jones's were drifting toward a dip in the ground where Jamie's mount had apparently found water. He'd stay now, had to, damn them. Whatever happens, Benedict had warned, stick together.

2

"Now," BENEDICT SAID, and with Oskar Mittenthaler and Ben Cantwell he strained upward on the fresh-cut pole. The wagon, which had been unloaded, tilted and creaked and was slowly lifted. The oxen, still yoked before it, were steadied by John Blue, the old Indian who drove Benedict's wagon.

Billy Black and Lee Cheatham worked the shattered wheel of the axle as the other men leaned forward, steadying the pole with their shoulders, digging their heels into the stony slope. Billy greased the hub and Lee rolled the spare wheel into place. They lifted it and pushed it into place. Lee Cheatham grabbed a spoke, spun the wheel and backed away.

"Easy now." Benedict grunted. The wagon settled down.

Cantwell walked off without a word to tend to his horse

9

which had drifted away to nibble at the clumps of grass under the tall trees.

"It's my fault," Benedict said to Mittenthaler. "I should have checked it back at the spring."

"You can't be ten places at once," Oskar Mittenthaler said. He was a sandy-haired man in his forties, of average size with an intelligent, sensitive look, an immigrant with a soft German accent. He was a master carpenter with two chests of fine tools in his wagon.

They both knew that if anyone was to blame for the accident it was Ben Cantwell who had volunteered to drive the wagon after Bill Grant died. Cantwell was a city man, and didn't know much about wagons or animals.

Theodosia Grant scraped up another handful of spilled topsoil, packing it around the roots of a grapevine cutting that had been bruised in the accident. While the men worked on the wheel, she'd been on her knees, retrieving the scattered roots and bulbs she'd nurtured since leaving home: grape cuttings and delicate seedlings of peach and pear and apple, bulbs and tubers of iris and tulip and lily, cans of seeds to plant in the new land: corn and beans, melons and sunflowers, squash, hollyhock, pumpkin, all manner and variety of living things.

She finished and stood up, a tall woman of thirty, not beautiful but even-featured and serene, with dark, windblown hair and skin turned brown by the long summer's sun. The death of her husband and the hardships of the journey had left no visible scars on her. She was normally outgoing and happy but at the moment her thoughts had turned inward and a few faint lines of worry creased her forehead. Her two sons, Patrick and Jesse, almost babies, had stopped playing and had crawled back into the wagon.

Benedict went to her.

"Where's Naomi?" he asked. She was Theodosia's seventeen-year-old niece who'd been sickly since the desert crossing. "I was afraid she was in the wagon."

"She's in the Silveras' wagon," Theodosia said. "Resting."

"You might see if she's up to walking, and the boys too. Country's getting rough . . . you can never tell now when a wagon will slide again or tip over."

"She'll walk with me," Theodosia said. Benedict didn't like to give orders but he had a deep sense of concern for all of them.

He was a man of average size in his middle years. Some accident had changed his left foot so that he walked with a slight limp. His was a farmer's face, the weathered skin pulled tight over the planes of cheek and jaw, the eyes narrowed from long years of sun and dust.

She glanced at his hands. They were large and well formed. Heavy work had not thickened the long fingers and when he lifted something, the knuckles tightened and made a straight line, a fist that was almost perfectly square. Long ago her mother had told her that a woman could tell a lot about a man by his hands. Maybe it was true. Benedict had good hands.

Benedict touched the brim of his hat and turned away to find his horse and continue up the trail.

Now, under the big trees, the party looked small and vulnerable, a handful of weary people struggling up a mountain where no wagons had ever gone before — and they had to get over, had to find a way up and over the mountain before the snow came. Seven wagons and a few single men with only their pack rolls and the animals they rode, like Lee Cheatham and Billy Black, the two wild boys from Ohio, and Ben Cantwell of St. Louis. And scouting ahead there were Webster Shaughnessey and young Jamie Mecom and Jones, the Mountain Man, seeking out and marking the best way up the unknown mountain.

When they'd split off from the main group to strike south for California, the group had seemed formidable; then, after the torture of the long desert crossing, most of them had voted to go over the mountain. Now, the sight of the small party made him wonder.

In the desert where there were only stunted bushes, they'd walked tall, casting long shadows — godlike beings passing through a hellish landscape. Now, moving up the sierra, they were slowly dwarfed by the raw and primal thrust of the mountain; boulders were gigantic; they and their wagons and animals insignificant. But they had to go on. It was too late in the year to continue south. They had to cross the sierra before winter struck.

3

DALLAS MECOM, sleeping in the back of his wagon, awoke when the creaking and rolling suddenly stopped. It was, Joseph told him from the driver's seat, an accident, a broken wheel, the Grant woman's wagon. They had to stop until it was fixed.

Dallas cursed softly at the black man and fell back on the tangle of buffalo robes, a handsome, blue-eyed, yellow-haired man of thirty, not tall but deep-chested and muscular. They'd fix the wheel without him. He was still goddamn tired from sitting up half the night guarding the stock. Benedict was so fired up about crossing the mountain — let him fix it.

Benedict was scared. He'd convinced most of the others to push over the mountain instead of continuing south; he was scared of winter, telling them they had to hurry to get across before snow came, even when Jones swore it was too early for snow. There was damn little chance they'd make it. You didn't just point yourself at a mountain with wagons and animals and women and expect to get over it. It would be smarter, he'd argued, to keep moving south, despite the lack of water, the threat of Indians. But Benedict had convinced the others to attempt a crossing.

He yawned and closed his eyes. The mountain air had a good tang to it anyway, clean and piny smelling. Missouri summers were hot with too much malaria, the winters bitter cold. And there was more law there now than a man needed. When he and Jamie got to California, they'd grab a piece of new land, plenty big, with lots of water; it'd be a new start for the Mecom tribe and sure as Christ they needed it . . .

He dozed off, thinking of Theodosia Grant. There was a measure of woman. Theodosia Grant was afraid of him, that much was certain, but it was a good sign: showed she knew he was a man.

There were shouts, the crack of Joseph's whip and the wagon lurched forward, shaking him out of his half-sleep. Most of the party was following Benedict now, doin' what he said, following him up the mountain — but things had a way of changin', people had a way of changin', changin' fast.

Joseph, the black man, talked to the four oxen pulling the wagon up the slope, a solid, powerfully built man with gray hair and eyes that seemed extra large and alert. He'd been born, as his father before him, on the original Mecom farm in Georgia. Then when the land gave out, he moved west with the family, moving three times before old Adam Mecom found a piece of land that he farmed until they buried him. Then Dallas and Jamie, the two youngest boys, got the California fever. They'd taken him and the wagon down to Independence and the rendezvous and headed west.

The goin' wasn't bad now but up ahead the trail would be steep and there'd be times again as in the mountains before the salt desert when extra yokes would have to be used to get them over bad spots. And maybe, like Mister Dallas kept saying, they'd have to leave everything, leave the wagons, leave the animals and go over the mountain with nothing at all.

Up ahead, Mister Cantwell was drivin' the Grant wagon, crackin' his whip, shoutin', pushin' the animals faster than was proper . . . Whenever there was a commotion there was Mister Cantwell from St. Louis, dressed in his city clothes, doin' most of the talkin' and none of the work. It was his fault that the wheel broke. Afterward Mister Benedict had cut the pole and he and Mittenthaler had put their backs under it and the two boys had put on the new wheel. But if you didn't look real careful you'd think Cantwell had done the thing himself . . .

He'd be a free man over the mountain. It was a fact, he'd be free and alone. Didn't seem possible but even Dallas admitted to it. When they got over the mountain, they'd be in Mexican land and he'd be jus' like the white men, get himself settled as a blacksmith, get away from Dallas.

15

Dallas wasn't good. Not like Jamie who was up ahead with the trapper and young Mr. Shaughnessey who, now and then when they were alone, talked about California and how he'd be free there under Mexican law and how things would be different. Didn't seem right or possible that Jamie and Dallas were brothers, born of the same woman, fathered by the same man. Dallas jus' naturally drew trouble to him but Jamie was a gentle boy, never caused trouble or got mixed up in it and maybe in this new place over the mountain Jamie too would break away and be free.

4

BENEDICT, RIDING HIS HORSE, saw the tree and stopped. It was almost too much to believe: a great living thing, thicker and taller than any he'd ever seen.

"*Godalmighty,*" he said aloud.

Then something moved, catching his eye: fear stabbed him but it was only Webster Shaughnessey standing next to a big rock, hands on hips, as if waiting for him, tall and trim, a young man of twenty-four with a hard Irish face, dressed in a threadbare black suit and Sunday hat, sunlight glinting on his eyeglasses. Of all the party, he had come the farthest, from somewhere along the Connecticut River. He had been to a college in Massachusetts, taught school for a year, and then heard about California.

"What's happened?" Benedict shouted. "Where's the others?" He kicked his horse forward.

"We're all here," Webster said. "Safe and sound."

"Indians?"

"No," Webster said. "We got here, stopped to look at
the tree. Then Jones unsaddled, said he wasn't going on,
said he was staying. I told him we best move but he
said no, said the wagons would stop here once everybody
saw this big tree."

Benedict sat frowning down on the other man. He'd
known that the Mountain Man was trouble the moment
he'd appeared out of the swirling white dust of the desert,
startling Theodosia who'd first seen him, a lone figure
coming toward them across the dead and shimmering
landscape . . .

"I tried to get him to move," Webster said, "but he said
no, he wasn't going. Said because there's water here, the
others would stay. Then Jamie turned on me, said he'd
stay too. I was going on alone but you told us to stick
together."

Benedict nodded. It was the truth, lame as it sounded.
Webster had a lot of sand in his craw, he never minced
words, never agreed with any of them just for the sake of
convenience; he wasn't trying to excuse himself or blame
Jones; he was just telling what had happened.

"You did the right thing," he said. He looked up at the
tree and felt the awesome power of the great trunk, the
sweeping majesty of its height. It was, he had to admit, a
fantastic and wonderful thing, but the sight of it was
mixed up with the anger within him. Now there was no
sure trail ahead. They'd have to stop.

He kicked his horse and rode past Webster, finding
Jones and Jamie Mecom sitting with their backs against

one of the high buttressing roots of the tree; it was cool in the shade and quiet, the clop of the horse's hooves muffled by the layer of pine needles. As he approached, Jamie stood up but Jones stayed where he was, whittling on a dead stick.

"We picked you up," he said to Jones. "Fed you. Gave you a horse. Now you're going against me."

The Mountain Man smiled up at him with crooked teeth.

"They'll want to camp here, Benedict. No sense in pushing on. Only have to come back. They'll stay here. You watch."

"You cost us half a day."

"There's good water here."

"We don't need water."

"They'll stop without your say-so," Jones said. "Dallas and the others."

Benedict studied him. Maybe Dallas had put him up to it, maybe not. Dallas didn't like him but there had never been any real trouble between them. But Dallas had seemed to find an ally in the Mountain Man. They'd both opposed his decision to cross the mountain. Now Jones had stopped him.

"Don't push me," he said.

Jones tossed the stick aside. Now the knife was a weapon.

"I'm stayin' here, Benedict. Nobody stoppin' you. Move on if that's your fancy."

Benedict turned to Jamie Mecom. "You told me you wanted to help, wanted to scout. First time out you quit."

The boy flushed. Everything was all turned around, all wrong. He liked Mister Benedict even if his brother didn't. And Jones was special — a real Mountain Man — but now he'd turned mean. Damn it all, he should have ridden on with Webster. He started to speak, to explain, but Benedict turned his horse and was moving away.

5

As EACH WAGON PULLED over the rise and onto the level ground below the tree, the men and the women and the children stopped talking and stared up at it. They would stop and make camp. No one heard Benedict give the order but Webster Shaughnessey and Jones were here and they were the trail-makers. The day's travel was over.

Oskar Mittenthaler looked upward, trying to glimpse the top of the tree which must be hundreds of meters high. In all Germany, in the Old World, there was no such tree, none so magnificent.

He spoke to his wife in German. "It is unbelievable."

"Yes," Anna said. It looked too big to be a living thing.

She was a quick, dark-haired woman of forty with light skin that never sunburned, filled with energy and optimism. Twenty years before she and Oskar had come from the Rhineland and settled in Missouri. Last spring they had sold their farm to their son-in-law, loaded their wagon, and joined the big party outside of Independence.

"How old, Oskar?"

"Hundreds of years," he said, "perhaps thousands."

They walked slowly toward the great tree to touch the rough bark, to walk between the buttressing knees, to circle it slowly, staring upward.

Naomi followed Theodosia and her two young sons, walking with Jamie Mecom.

"We couldn't believe it," Jamie said. They both nodded, not looking at him, walking as fast as they could on the slippery pine needles.

"It doesn't look real," Naomi said. She was a light-boned girl of seventeen, slim and vibrant, brown from a summer in the sun. She took Jamie's hand and looked into his face — dark browed and handsome, not hard and strong like his brother's but almost delicate, with a thin nose and large deep-set eyes.

"It's real enough," he said.

"It's beautiful — and we're the first to see it. Nobody's ever been this way before."

"Indians," Jamie said. "Diggers. They must have seen it but nobody else, that's for sure."

"I just can't believe it."

She stooped down and picked up one of the big pine cones that littered the ground.

"Jones said he never saw one bigger," Jamie said. "And he's been everywhere, all his life, trappin' and huntin'."

*

John Van Sciber turned to his wife and reached for her hand, a frail, aristocratic man of fifty with hair that was totally white.

"The patriarch," he said. "And we've discovered it — we'll be famous."

He spoke slowly, enunciating each word in a casual, cultured voice. The others knew almost nothing about John Van Sciber except that he was recently married. For the most part he kept to himself and never spoke about his past. What they saw was contradictory: a man who bore one of the great Colonial names of early New York, obviously well educated but moving west with them in an ordinary wagon and commonplace equipment.

Betty Van Sciber nodded. If she'd only brought her drawing paper and fine pencils she'd try to sketch it — a great thick trunk rising up as if it were made of stone rather than living wood, a tree so tall that . . .

"Wait," her husband said. "I'll get a rope. We'll measure its girth."

"No," she said. "Not now, John. Stay with me."

She was twenty years younger than her husband, small, almost petite, with butter-colored hair and dark eyes. She'd married John Van Sciber three weeks after they'd met when he'd already decided to go west.

Gideon Hassler, farmer and preacher, fought the urge to kneel.

"What kinda tree, Pa?" asked ten-year-old Lucas.

"Don't know, son," Gideon said. "Some kind of pine or fir or evergreen."

Long ago he had been tall and robust but time and

work and age and the Missouri fevers had worn him down until now, at forty-five, he was thin and bent, his long face seamed and leathery.

He began to create a sermon: the tree had lived and grown for a thousand years because it was . . . because it nourished itself on the heavenly sun and the sweet waters under the earth, because no man had seen it, coveted it . . .

"It's beautiful," his wife Lydia said, almost to herself. Childbirth and years of hard work had thickened her body but she was still young-looking and undaunted by the hardships of the long journey. Lucas was her youngest. Ben had died of fever almost two years ago and Dan had joined the Volunteers and was probably down in Texas now with Zack Taylor, fighting Mexicans.

"We should gather and pray," Gideon said.

"No," Lydia said gently. "Not now, Gideon, not now."

There was no need to kneel here, to read from the Book. The tree itself made them small and humble; no words could add to the power of the place.

Manuel Silvera, a handsome man in his middle thirties, hugged his wife and daughter, squeezing them to him, his lean dark face aglow with excitement. This was the first sign of California, a land where everything grew twice as fast as any other place. A land of warm days and rich soil, land of their people.

His wife Inez nodded, lost in wonder, a small, sturdy woman with a round face and large Aztec eyes. They had joined the Americans along the trail, unable to return to

Santa Fe because of the war. It was best, Manuel had explained, to join the party of Americans, better to travel in safety while they could, to move westward. They had sold their horses and had the gold coins hidden in the bottom of their wagon. In the new place they would take what land they wanted and breed fine horses.

Nilda, fifteen, slim and excitable, stepped ahead of her parents, then turned back.

"I can't believe it."

Her father smiled, nodding, understanding too that there was something about the great tree that was strange and unreal.

"It's only a dream," he said. "Close your eyes and when you open them it will be gone, vanished."

"No," the girl said. "Don't say that, don't think that," and she left them and moved close to her magical tree.

And at last they all stood before the great tree, silent and alone, each of them, in wonder and humility.

6

BENEDICT WATCHED HIS HORSE drink water that trickled from the moss-filled cracks in a slab of flat, gray rock. The animal lifted its head and began to nose about the bank eating the clumps of grass that grew in the dappled shade. The horse, like all the others, was thin and footsore, and it was good to see him rest. Suddenly the animal turned, looked at him as if reading his thoughts, then trotted away to join the other horses.

The spring was south of the big tree — three or four hundred feet — at about the same elevation. The wagons had stopped on the level ground midway between the big tree and the spring. Benedict stood now and watched the party gathered at the base of the tree and knew it was a sight they'd remember to their dying days, a portent of the new land, big and lusty, unspoiled by older generations of men. The tree made him feel like a boy again, filled with the excitement of discovery; maybe someday there'd be a town close to this spot and people would walk here on long summer evenings to be alone, to think, to rest their souls . . .

But he couldn't enjoy the tree; it had stopped them in a way nothing else had, it had caused them to lose time they couldn't afford. This morning there had been a thin film of ice on the water in the bottom of his kettle; tonight it would be colder.

Behind him a twig snapped and he turned. John Blue was staring at him. The old Indian, normally impassive, was visibly upset.

"What is it, John?"

The old face was cracked and crinkled like the clay at the bottom of a dried-up waterhole, a face haughty with old age.

"No stop," he said. "We go, we go . . ."

Benedict shrugged. "There's no sure trail now — that damn Mountain Man quit on us. I don't want to move them without scouting ahead."

John Blue waved a withered hand toward the tree and the others, dismissing them.

"Move," he said. "Make all move."

A beautiful place, Benedict thought, if only they'd earned it; if only they'd made a decent day's move.

"Go," the old man repeated. "Bad camp. Make all go. By and by too late . . ."

Benedict nodded. The old man was prodding him toward a decision he'd already half made. He took one last look at the horses, knowing they wouldn't wander too far from the water, then walked past John Blue, toward the tree, to Ben Cantwell who stood, arms folded on his chest, a cigar in his mouth, gazing upward, lost in thought.

"Ben, I want to talk to you."

Cantwell lowered his head and stared at him. He was an even-featured man of medium height; his trim mustache and worn but well-tailored black suit set him apart from most of the other men. He had a habit of looking at people with a slight frown, as if he were studying them, as if he never quite believed what they were saying.

"I'm going on," Benedict said. "I can't sit here the rest of the day looking at this tree. I'm going to scout ahead and I'd like you along with me. Soon as I eat I'll be pushing on until the light fails. If the trail's good we'll make camp. Wagons can move out in the morning."

Cantwell was studying him, eyes narrowed, cigar tilted upward. He'd been in and out of several businesses, Benedict knew, and involved in politics back in Missouri, claimed to be a close friend of Doniphan in St. Louis.

"Will you come?" Benedict asked.

"I'll come," Cantwell said. "Be glad to."

"Good."

"Just the two of us," Cantwell said. It was a statement but also a question.

"I'm going to ask young Mecom," Benedict said, turning away.

"Why in hell did they stop?"

"It was Jones," Benedict said. "He wouldn't move out and Jamie stuck with him — figuring it was the best thing, maybe. Anyway, he's allowed a mistake or two, a young fellow like him."

28

Cantwell started to speak, then stopped. Maybe Benedict wasn't as open and simple as he appeared, maybe Benedict was up to something — hitting back at Dallas Mecom by making a friend of his younger brother. Dallas had never liked Benedict and they'd usually stayed clear of one another, but since Jones had joined them Dallas was talking openly against Benedict's leadership, telling others that they'd never make it over the mountain, that they should turn back and move south.

"Why not Webster?" he asked.

"I want him here. With the wagons. He'll get them moving in the morning."

Cantwell nodded. Webster would look after Theodosia Grant's wagon especially, be around her while Benedict was away.

"I'm ready when you are," he said.

Benedict left. He turned back to the tree. It was a California tree — big and beautiful and unspoiled, everything they said it was. This one single tree could provide enough wood for God only knew how many houses; it was too big to handle but the ones around it, most of them on the slope, were huge by any normal index — a wealth of fine clean timber.

Trees were fine to look at but in the end they had to be cut to generate wealth and power for those willing to gamble their time, their capital.

7

THEODOSIA GRANT'S FIRST CONCERN was her plants. In the desert she hadn't used the brackish water, for it was bitter, filled with unknown salts which would poison the delicate living things. She'd kept them alive with daily measured drops from her supply of drinking water. If the crossing had taken another day most of them would have dried up and perished.

After the desert the party had rested, spending three days near a small spring that they drained dry every day. Now there was an abundance of clear sparkling water welling up out of the mountainside, enough for all the animals and people, cold water for their moldy water kegs and canteens.

While Webster and Naomi unyoked the oxen she and her two small sons hurried to the spring and returned with a bucket and two cans, filling each earthen pot, each box and tin, until every plant was flooded, until water dripped on the ground beneath the wagon.

She knelt down and put an arm around each of the boys.

"Are we going to live here?" Jesse asked.

"Just for today and tonight," she said. "We'll leave in the morning, go up the big mountain. Soon we'll be over it."

"To our new farm," Patrick explained to the younger boy. He was most like his father, stocky and well formed, with blue eyes and raven black hair. She hugged him closer and kissed his ear.

"That's right," Theodosia said. "Now listen to me. I want both of you to find me some of the pine cones that have fallen out of the tree. Will you do that?"

"For the fire?" Jesse asked.

"No," she said. "For the seeds, the little seeds inside of them. You and Patrick find me some and we'll put them in a box and let them dry. They'll open up a little at a time and the seeds will fall out and next spring we'll plant them."

Jesse nodded. "We'll have little trees."

"Yes. Someday when we're old we'll have a special tree that came from the seeds and it'll make us remember this day — the finding of this wonderful tree."

She stood up, rubbing the small of her back, watching the two boys run up the slope searching the ground. She thought of Benedict, up ahead with Ben Cantwell and Jamie Mecom, scouting the best way for the wagons. When night came they'd be alone up there, the first time any of them had been separated from the party overnight. She looked around: the campsite was sunny and parklike now, filled with the sound of laughter, but no civilized people had ever been here; there were no marks on the trees, no remains of old fires, nothing.

She began to unload the things she'd need to cook, reminding herself to warn Naomi and the two boys to stay close to the wagon. Mr. Benedict was gone; there were three less men in camp now and when the sun went down the glade would become a dark and primeval place.

8

THE OXEN WERE FREED from their heavy yokes, watered at the spring, then herded into a bowllike depression close to the last wagon. There was little danger that they would wander off, for there was no forage and they were foot-sore and exhausted. Silvera and Joseph had encircled the depression with rope tied taut from one tree to the next. In addition, when darkness came, a guard would watch over them.

All of the horses and the four mules were tethered on a line at one end of the makeshift corral. Silvera's stallion was led in last. It was the finest horse most of them had ever seen. Silvera was a breeder of horses and the animal was his future. He fed it grain and curried it at the end of each day. At night he kept it tied to the tailgate of his wagon.

Each family cooked and ate a meager meal and the

women turned to their chores. The men began to drift back to the tree. John Van Sciber was first, joining Jones, who'd eaten with Dallas Mecom. The scrawny Mountain Man was half-asleep, his head propped up against one of the roots that extended from the bole of the great evergreen.

Van Sciber held out the half-gallon jug of Missouri whiskey he'd brought from his wagon. Jones took the jug, sat up, and drank.

"They said even you've never seen a tree the size of this," Van Sciber said.

Jones nodded. "Seen a piece of this country. Seen a tree or two in my time, yassah. Big fellas — but nothin' this size."

Van Sciber was excited. "Seems like we oughta name it or something since we're the ones found it."

Jones wiped his mouth. "Nobody's ever gonna see here again," he said. "Not in my time, your time."

"We could put it on a map," Van Sciber said. "People might come lookin' for it. Who saw it first?"

"Mecom," Jones said. He handed the jug to the other man.

"The Mecom Tree," Van Sciber said. "Or maybe name it after Benedict."

"Names don't mean nuthin'," Jones said.

"They do and they don't," Van Sciber said, then realized the great gulf between himself and the half-wild Mountain Man and quickly raised the jug to his mouth.

Lee Cheatham and Billy Black came carrying their rifles and squatted down with them.

They were both nineteen, dark-haired, good-looking boys who'd grown up together in a small quiet town in Ohio. Lee Cheatham was an even six feet, lean and quick and hard to anger. Billy was a few inches shorter, heavier, more strongly built. They were dead shots and had done most of the hunting for the party. When the war started they'd left to join the army, to go to Texas and fight Mexicans. Instead they'd got the California fever and joined the original party in Independence.

"We're looking for deer," Billy said.

He pushed back his wide-brimmed U.S. Cavalry hat that he'd bought from a drunken trooper near Fort Bridger.

"We sort of figured you might like to come," Lee said.

"Boys," Jones said. "I'd tag along but this old hoss's got a mind to rest up. I'll 'spect you'll find all the meat you can carry, soon as you get away from our stink. Start by the spring and work south."

"We'll give you first crack at it," Billy said.

Lee Cheatham nodded. Jones would take it anyway; better than any of them, he knew how to butcher.

9

GIDEON HASSLER ON HIS WAY to collect firewood came with his ten-year-old son Lucas and stood listening to the others talk. At first young Lucas, holding an axe, stood beside his father, listening to the talk, then he drifted away.

He stared up at the tree, then went close to it, braced his feet and swung the axe. It hit straight on and bounced back, throwing him off balance. He swung again at an angle and the axe blade sliced into the thick, shaggy bark. He swung again and again until a section of the rough bark fell away.

The men stopped talking, pointed at him and began laughing. It was a sight. A small boy attacking the gigantic tree with an axe almost too heavy for him to swing.

"Wait'll we get clear!" Van Sciber shouted.

"He's got the right idea," Billy Black said, reaching for the whiskey jug. "Pick a big one or nothin' at all."

36

"You raised him right," Jones said to Gideon.

Dallas Mecom came up the slope, walking slowly, watching the boy swinging the axe. Someday the tree had to go down, even if it'd been there for hundreds of years, maybe a thousand. Years and years from now some mealy-mouthed hire-out city men would come along and saw the bastard down. It'd be something, to watch her fall . . .

As he passed behind the boy the axe stuck fast in the fibrous bark. The boy pulled, too hard and off balance; his sweaty hands slipped on the smooth handle and he fell down. Dallas stopped, looked at the boy and at the axe. Then he stepped forward, pulled the axe free, holding it out to the boy who sat on the ground, winded and red faced. Lucas shook his head. He'd had enough.

Dallas swung the axe, freeing a chip that went spinning away. He swung again and again, changing his stance, getting the feel of the axe, clearing away the mutilated bark, biting into the wood. After a day of sleeping and waiting he found familiar pleasure in feeling the sharp blade bite . . .

"Take her down, Dallas," Billy Black shouted, the whiskey jug on his shoulder. "God*damn!*"

"No," Lee Cheatham said. "Leave it be."

Dallas stopped, looked up. *Give this bastard a taste of the steel before the mealy-mouths come.*

"Time for a drink," Van Sciber shouted. When Dallas Mecom got his teeth into something, you had to shake him loose. Dallas dropped the axe and walked to them and took the jug. He drank but his eyes followed the tree up and up; others had seen it before him but he'd been the first to cut into the clean wood.

Naomi and Webster Shaughnessey walked up the rise. "I'm glad you stopped here," Naomi said.

Webster frowned. He'd told her the truth about what had happened when they'd sighted the tree but already she'd forgotten the most important thing.

"I wanted to go on," he said. "I told you that. It was old Jones who wouldn't move. And then Jamie said he'd stay with Jones."

"I'm glad anyway," she said lightly. "There's no need to hurry so, is there?"

"Benedict thinks so."

She shrugged and walked on. Mr. Benedict was a fine man, quiet and always worrying about the rest of them, about Aunt Theodosia, forgetting half the time to look after his own things, forgetting to eat, never getting a proper night's sleep.

She stopped and looked up at the tree. Later, when she wrote in her diary, she'd try to describe it . . . *a thing so great, so alive . . . I wanted to kneel and pray, to thank . . .*

Webster was showing more interest in her recently, that's what Aunt Theo said. Webster — he'd been born on Daniel Webster's birthday and his parents had given him the name — was a special kind of person; he'd been one of the few men who ever noticed Aunt Theo's plants, who didn't seem uneasy talking about flowers. He was interested in all things, always learning a little here and a little there, something about horses from Manuel Silvera or how Oskar Mittenthaler replaced a broken wheelspoke.

He wasn't much older than Jamie Mecom but he wore city clothes and he'd been to a university and he never read his Bible or joined them at Sunday prayers. And back at the spring he'd had long arguments about the war with Ben Cantwell and Billy Black, telling them that American soldiers had no right in Mexico just because President Polk wanted to make a name for himself. And now Webster was becoming interested in her and it was only natural that Jamie should resent him.

They began to circle the tree, moving out of sight of the others. Suddenly they stopped.

John Van Sciber, holding a wooden mallet and a chisel, stood close to the tree staring at something. They drew closer and saw that he had cut away a square of bark and inscribed his name and the date in the bare wood.

J. VAN SCIBER

1846

He turned to them, sweat glistening on his face, his bare arms and clothes flecked with curls of wood and bark.

"It'll give somebody a surprise one of these days," he said. He moved back a few paces and looked at his work from another angle.

"It's very nice," Naomi said, but it was an automatic response and she wished that she hadn't spoken at all. She wanted to smooth out the deep savage cuts, paste back the bark and leave the tree as before. Now it was mutilated. It would never be quite the same again. He'd desecrated the tree, violated her memory of the place.

Aunt Theo had once said that there was something wrong with John Van Sciber — strange that he, who bore one of the great old names of America, was with them at all; now he'd committed a stupid and childish act.

"This way they'll know we were here," Van Sciber said.

"Who?" Webster asked.

Van Sciber flushed. "Why, people. Those who come this way next."

Webster shrugged. It didn't seem possible that anyone else would ever come this exact way through these remote mountains.

Naomi was walking away and Webster followed her, leaving Van Sciber studying his name cut deeply into the fresh wood of the ancient tree.

10

Two hours later young Lucas Hassler, playing hide-and-seek with the two little Grant boys, came to the tree and hid breathless in the cavelike fire scar. Long ago, his father had said, a fire had eaten into the base of the tree and the flames had swept upward, making the tall, wedge-shaped scar. There was no one around now; the day was almost over and everyone had gathered around the cooking fires on the flatland below where the wagons stood.

He looked up at the dead blackened wood around him, saw that he could climb upward, that he could do something that none of the others had done. He kicked off his shoes, peeled off his ragged stockings, and began to climb upward, his feet finding purchase both in the rough bark and in the splintered, black wood, his knees enclosing the lip of new growth that curled inward in a natural effort to cover the dead wood.

The wagons would leave in the morning and follow Mr. Benedict's trail and he'd be the only one who'd climbed the tree, even a little of it. Dallas Mecom had taken his axe and cut into the wood and Mr. Van Sciber had even cut his name into it, but none of them had climbed it, just him. His legs started to tremble but he kept going; he was strong, even for ten, and he could climb on except he mustn't look down because it might scare him . . .

It would be wonderful if he could climb all the way to the top and see the eagle's nest. He pictured himself finding eggs in the nest, taking one, bringing it back down to keep warm, under one of the settin' hens that was caged in the Silveras' wagon. He'd have a baby pet eagle, something nobody else ever had, an eagle that he'd train to come swooping down out of the sky to his outstretched arm.

He felt the wood break, ever so slightly; he froze in fear, his heart pumping extra loud, his eyes stinging with sweat that he couldn't wipe away. He'd come too far. He'd have to start edging back down. As he'd climbed, the lip of wood had become thinner until now it was mostly bark covering the blackened dead wood under it.

He took a deep breath and began to move down but the shifting of his weight split the weakened wood. He fell clutching a long sliver of wood, turned in the air, hit the ground to roll awkwardly, to lie still and dead.

11

GIDEON HASSLER WALKED down the slope, his long face streaked with tears, the body of his dead son in his arms. He walked toward the others with a strange, stiff, measured step.

"He fell," he said, speaking to all of them.

"Dear God," Anna Mittenthaler said. "Dear God . . ."

"Tryin' to crawl up. Inside that old fire scar. Wood's rotten . . ." His voice cracked and he began to cry again.

Joseph went to him and held out his thick black arms and took the small body. He walked toward the Hassler wagon and Gideon followed, wiping his tears away with the back of his hand.

Webster Shaughnessey felt sick. Little Lucas was a bright boy, a good boy. He would have grown to manhood in the new place, in California. Jones, damn his hide . . . he'd made them stop.

He turned to Theodosia Grant who stood with her two small sons beside her.

"I feel responsible for this," he said quietly.

She stared at him, her face taut with strain, her large eyes brimming with tears. She shook her head back and forth again and again as if to say, *Don't say that, don't ever say that* . . .

Inez Silvera crossed herself and looked at Dallas Mecom and Jones. There was so much evil in the world — so many bad men and yet God had struck down this last son of a good and gentle woman, a good and gentle man.

In the gloom of a dying day the air was suddenly heavy, the trees dark and threatening, closing in on them. Betty Van Sciber turned away and began to weep. They were so few, the mountain so vast and savage — she was afraid now for herself, for all of them; they were exhausted from months of travel, they were lost.

John Blue stared upward at the tree and spoke words in his own ancient language. It was the first tree in the world. It had sprouted through the hard cold earth in the long-ago time when the world was bare, when his people lived like animals. Now the Whites had cut the tree, and to warn them it had taken the boy. If they did not leave, others would die.

They ate quiet suppers and gathered around the Mittenthalers' fire, building it up with dead wood. After a time, when no one else organized the guard in Benedict's absence, Webster Shaughnessey circulated among the men, avoiding Jones and Dallas Mecom, and put Lee Cheatham in the corral with the animals, and John Van Sciber around the wagons.

Night began to close around them and a chill mist was rising. The women rummaged by candlelight through the musty trunks and bags to find warmer clothing. They were used to warm summer nights, the desert heat. Now it was cold.

The Night

12

BENEDICT CRUMPLED a handful of twigs and dropped them on the gray coals, blew gently, and leaned back on his heels as the flames burst upward, licking on the powdered bark and decayed wood. It was still night but the black sky was streaked with the first slivers of dawn's light.

He was exhausted and wondered if he had slept. All he could remember was lying with the heat of the glowing fire on his face, thinking of Theodosia Grant and sometime during the long night he admitted to himself that he was here because of her. When the main party broke up at the river he'd joined the smaller group, telling himself that California was closer, less crowded than Oregon, forcing the truth from his mind. Now, under his breath, he said, *Yes, Theodosia. I joined them to be with you* . . .

Cantwell stirred under his buffalo robe and sat up, half-asleep.

"Anything wrong?"

"I want to move on a bit," Benedict said. "No reason for you to come. Get your sleep. I'm going on."

Cantwell grunted and got up, poured water from his canteen into a battered copper kettle, set it in the fire. They'd ridden on until darkness halted them. Ahead the mountain rose sharply.

Jamie Mecom sat up yawning, shivering. "What's goin' on, Mr. Benedict?"

"You stay here," Benedict said. "With Ben. I'm going on but I'll try to get back before the wagons get here. If not, hold them here."

"I'll go with you," Cantwell said.

"Get your rest, Ben."

Cantwell dropped a handful of coffee beans into the water.

"No reason why the two of us have to stay here," he said.

"I'd be glad to have you along, Ben, but it'd be best for you to get your sleep."

"I'd like to go with you," Cantwell said. He stood up and stretched. He was dog-tired and needed the sleep but he couldn't let Benedict go on alone and find a way over the ridge — if there was a way. If they were forced back down the mountain they'd choose a new captain. Dallas Mecom had a following but he was crude and unpredictable. Webster was too young. Jones wasn't one of them. Hassler couldn't lead men. They'd pick a new captain and it would be him.

"You stay here then," Benedict said to Jamie. "If the

rest of them get here before we get back tell them to wait."

"Yes, sir," Jamie said. "I'll sure tell them." He'd never fail Mr. Benedict again. Never again.

13

ON THE SLOPE a hundred feet below the big tree there was a gray rock as high and as wide as one of the wagons and around it the needle-cushioned forest floor was level and sunlit. It was here that Gideon and Lydia Hassler had chosen to bury their son.

Lydia listened to the last of her husband's eulogy for Lucas and then stood quietly as the others came to mumble expressions of condolence and walk back to their wagons.

She was all cried out now and nothing seemed real: Gideon's long, big-nosed face was out of focus, the lines and deep wrinkles reminding her of a rough piece of country, furrowed by eroded gullies, that they'd passed through the first month on the trail. Lucas had liked that place but no one else; there was no forage and the oxen had bloodied their tender hooves on the loose gravel.

The others were gone and she stood with Gideon staring at the neat pile of stones that the men had put on the fresh earth. She was so tired, so heartbroken weary from moving that if she could die by wishing, she'd die and join poor Lucas . . .

Always moving. That was Gideon, as full of work and good intentions as any man but with a restlessness eating at him. They'd sold the first Kentucky farm that Gideon had cleared and tamed to move south. Then they'd gone north to Ohio, then west, like there was a magnet pulling them on. No sooner settled and comfortable than Gideon would get the movin' fever . . . and now she was old and weary and had buried another boy and they were still pushin' to the west.

Webster Shaughnessey stood with most of the men around Mittenthaler's fire. Now he took his watch and snapped it open, seeing the inscription on the back of the case:

> *To our son Webster on his twenty-first*
> *birthday, January 18, 1843*
> *Remember us*
> *Your loving father and mother*

He looked up the mountain; they'd be late now and Benedict, waiting somewhere up ahead, would begin to worry about them. It was almost nine o'clock.

"Sooner we move out, the better," he said quietly.

Mittenthaler nodded. It would be another hour before they'd be ready, before the oxen were yoked, the wagons packed. It was a great pity. If they hadn't stopped to admire the tree the Hassler boy would be alive.

"I'm stayin'," Dallas Mecom said. They'd barely spoken since they'd left Missouri; Webster smelled of cities and schools and highfalutin talk. No sonofabitch like that was goin' to tell him anything.

Webster looked across the fire, scowling, wondering if the other man was joking.

"Stayin' here another day," Dallas went on. "Good water. Rest for my poor animals. Figure I can catch up with you tomorrow with none of you in my way."

"You've got to go," Webster said. "We agreed on that back at the river. We all stick together."

Dallas shrugged and smiled and looked at Jones.

"Can't shoot a man for changing his mind now, can you?"

"I'll stick with you," Jones said. "Keep you company. Rest these old bones."

"We need you, Dallas," Webster said. "And your animals. There'll be hard goin' ahead. We're a party, not a bunch of wagons."

Dallas shrugged and looked past him, to the tree. He'd been thinking about it most of the night, unable to sleep.

"We ain't goin'," Jones said. "That's the end of it."

Billy Black squatted down and tossed a pine cone into the flames. "I say we all stay put for the rest of the day. Damn it, Webster, a man's got a right to a little rest, ain't he?"

"It's not a matter of right," Webster said. "We don't

have the time. We just rested three days. Now we've
got to move." He looked at John Van Sciber.

"It might be fittin' and respectful, Webster, to hold on
here for the rest of the day," Van Sciber said. He'd find
a nice clean board, carve LUCAS HASSLER in it, and the
dates that bracketed his short life.

"Oskar?"

"I'll come," Mittenthaler said, but he knew that
Webster could never convince them to move. He was
educated. In Europe a man like Webster would be listened to but here in the wilderness, in the *Urwald,* among
Dallas Mecom and some of the rest he was ignored, barely
tolerated.

"Cheatham don't want to move," Billy Black said.
"He'll want to stay and hunt."

"And these greasers too," Dallas said. "Them people
ain't the hurryin' sort."

He was defeated, Webster knew. They'd made up their
minds to stay and nothing he could say or do would
change them. The desert crossing had taken the starch
out of them; they were slack and slow now, resigned to
long delays, lost days.

Benedict was the only one who could pull them together. There was always the feeling that his judgment
was good, that he was right about things, even about the
mountain and the necessity of getting over it as fast as
possible.

"You're wrong," he said. "All of you. And you know
it. You're defying a man who's up there on the mountain
trying to find a way. Benedict didn't want to be captain

55

but you elected him and now you've got to respect him, not defy him."

"We're not defying him," Van Sciber said. "He's a good man but we just don't see all this hurryin'."

"It's late," Webster said. "Remember what Bentley said back at the river about the snow. It comes early in these mountains and if we fiddle around and get trapped we're finished."

"Too damn early for snow," Jones said. "I tole you that a hundred times now."

Webster walked away from them, looking up at the great sweep of the tree against the morning sky, wondering how it affected the others. If there was no danger, he'd like to stay too, just to sit and look at the tree.

He went to the Grant wagon where Theodosia and Naomi were getting ready to go. Jesse and Patrick were pouring water on the sputtering fire.

"We're not moving out," he said.

The two women stared at him.

"Dallas and Jones and Van Sciber and the rest of them. They won't move." He looked down at the sodden smoking embers. "They're going to stay here the rest of the day."

"Why?" Theodosia said. "I don't understand."

"I don't know," he said, looking up. "They've all got reasons — but it's something else, like they were in on some secret; something they knew that I didn't."

"Is it because of Lucas Hassler?" Naomi asked.

"No," Webster said. "It's Dallas, him and Jones. Tryin' to buck Benedict, I think. Tryin' to make him quit. Maybe that's what's behind it."

"That's terrible," Naomi said. All men seemed to do was fight each other.

"We'll go without them," Theodosia said. Dallas Mecom and Jones — she was afraid of them. For herself. For Naomi.

"Mittenthaler'll move on," Webster said. "And the Hasslers; I'm sure they would. And Lee Cheatham and the Silveras — but Benedict wouldn't want it. We've got to stick together whatever happens."

"We should do something," Theodosia said. Her two sons had run off, chasing each other around one of the trees.

"I'm going to ride up and find Benedict," Webster said. "He's up there waiting for us and it's best I get to him as fast as I can."

"Couldn't Billy Black go?" Theodosia asked. "If you leave . . ."

"He's in with them," Webster said. "Cheatham would go, I think, he's got more sense than Billy, only he's off hunting."

Theodosia took a deep breath and turned away to compose herself, closing her eyes for one instant, trying to remember her husband's face but seeing instead Gideon Hassler's with tears running down his cheeks, looking down at his dead son. She was afraid. Something was happening that she couldn't understand. Something, unseen and remorseless, that was all around them like the mists that were forming around the giant tree.

14

GIDEON HASSLER LEFT his wife and walked around the big stone, away from the grave, heading directly up the slope toward the tree where he could be alone.

He stopped some ten feet from the base. Something glinted in the churn of pine needles and he came toward it, saw that it was his axe, the axe that Lucas had swung at the tree. He picked it up, the heft and contour of the smooth handle familiar, an old tool but recently sharpened.

He walked on, swinging the axe, letting it turn in his hand. He came to the notch that Dallas had cut in the tree when he'd taken the axe from Lucas. His eyes moved upward and he wondered about the eagle that the others had seen, the white-headed bird that had its nest among the great branches.

"Go ahead," Dallas said. "Cut it."

He dropped his head, surprised, thinking he'd been alone. There was a peculiar mocking smile on Dallas's face. As if he'd been waiting by the tree, waiting for him . . .

"Cut it," Dallas repeated. "That's what you want, isn't it?"

Gideon shook his head. "No . . ."

"You hate this tree."

"No . . . you can't hate a tree."

"I'll help you."

Gideon stared at the other man, realizing now that he too had an axe.

"It killed your boy."

"You can't think that way."

"We'll cut it," Dallas said softly, moving closer. "You and me. The others too . . ."

"No," Gideon said. "Tree's got nothin' to do with it."

Dallas was in front of him.

Cut it damn you . . .

Gideon stared at the wide blue eyes, the long yellow hair, the thick pulsating vein that stood out on Dallas's forehead. He felt sick and vaguely afraid. He dropped the axe, stepped back and walked away.

Dallas felt the sharp edge of the axe blade with his thumb, smiling to himself, kicked away the loose pine needles to find a proper stance. He swung the axe, feeling the handle shiver as the blade cut into the bark, then swung again and again, building up a rhythm until his body was perfectly poised, until the work was almost effortless, the axe no longer an alien tool, but merging with his body, becoming a part of it. Man that didn't like sweatin' work wasn't a total man, didn't understand that choppin' wasn't work, that watching the chips fly and smelling raw wood was a fine thing — and cutting the tree was like killing a great animal, like getting the biggest elk, the biggest bear.

Below, the men around the fire, hearing the sound of the axe, looked up and frowned at the sight of Dallas, dwarfed by the distance, attacking the giant tree.

Lee Cheatham and Joseph, guided by the sound of the chopping, came down the slope, a deer carcass hanging from a thick pole between them. They had left a little after dawn, excusing themselves from Lucas Hassler's burial, trying to find some game before the party moved out.

Van Sciber saw them first and shouted. The others came hurrying. It was the first fresh meat in several days.

Jones and Silvera ducked under the pole and took the burden, carrying it toward the tree. Dallas Mecom, concentrating on his chopping, didn't notice them until they dropped the bloody animal.

"Cheatham finally got some meat," Van Sciber said. "A feast now, a real feast."

"Start the fire here," Jones said. "Away from the wagons, away from the damn women."

Lee Cheatham, still carrying his rifle, walked toward the tree, toward Dallas. He stood scowling at the raw wound in the tree, the deep V-shaped cut.

"You shouldn't have done that."

Dallas held the axe.

"Done what?"

"Cut the tree."

"Why the hell not?"

"It's a special tree, Dallas . . . biggest tree in the country, accordin' to Jones. You got no right to jus' walk up and start cuttin' it."

"Who says so?"

"I say so," Lee said. "Anybody with common sense. You went and ruined it."

"Get the hell away from me, Cheatham. I feel like doin' somethin' I do it."

"You had no right," Lee said.

He turned and walked back to the others, staring at the tiny fire that Van Sciber had started.

"First you didn't move out," he said. "Now Dallas is cuttin' the tree. What started this crazy chopping?"

Billy Black shrugged. "Dallas just started. All by himself . . ."

"Why didn't you stop it, Billy?"

Billy tilted his trooper's hat back on his head. He didn't understand why Lee was so damned upset.

Lee turned to Van Sciber. "Where's Mittenthaler?"

"Working on his wagon."

Jones was on his knees now, starting to butcher the bloody carcass with his razor-sharp knife.

"I thought you'd have moved out by now," Lee said.

"We decided to stay," Van Sciber said.

"It's a damn fool thing," Lee said. "Stayin' here. Benedict's expecting us."

"Webster rode off to tell him," Billy said.

Lee turned to him.

61

"You should have moved," he said. "Stayin' here don't make any sense at all."

Dallas stopped chopping. They all looked up as he came toward them. He held the axe before Joseph.

"You chop," he said to the black man.

"Damn it all, Dallas," Lee shouted. "Leave that tree alone."

Dallas dropped the axe and swung toward him, suddenly taut, crouching slightly, ready to fight.

"Shut your mouth, Cheatham, or I'll knock you silly."

Jones pulled his bloody knife from the meat.

"You two gonna fight, back off a piece."

"No need for fighting," Van Sciber said easily, standing up from his fire and moving toward them. "What we need, gentlemen, is firewood . . ."

Lee Cheatham stared at Dallas, then turned and walked away. Dallas was older and stronger and mean tempered; there was a story that he'd killed a man back in Missouri. If they fought, Dallas would beat him. And when it came down to cases, the tree was standing here, just as much Dallas's as anyone else's.

Benedict would settle it. He and Dallas were alike in a lot of ways. Stubborn, both of them. Independent as hell. Dallas was the kind most of them would like to be — nothing scared him and he was good-looking and full of hell. But Benedict was a better man. Quiet and steady. Never jumped into something in a hurry, never backed off from something that had to be done.

Behind him, Joseph picked up the axe and went to the tree and began to chop.

15

BENEDICT AND CANTWELL slipped off their horses without taking their eyes away from the sheer wall of gray rock that blocked their way. It was thirty feet high, running along the mountain as far as they could see.

"Looks bad," Cantwell said.

It was the end. He took the reins from Benedict and led both horses away to nibble at a patch of brown, wilted grass.

Benedict stared up at the rock barrier, wordless and ashamed. He walked forward and sat down on a slab of granite. The wagons were pulling up the mountain, moving up to where Jamie waited and it was all for nothing. Worse. They were almost out of food, out of time. They'd be forced to go back down to the flatland and move south — *damn the mountain* . . .

He was defeated, stopped by the granite wall, feeling

suddenly alone as he had once before since they'd started — the night Blackie had vanished . . .

"What do we do now?" Cantwell asked.

Benedict turned, his face drawn with fatigue, black hat pushed back on his head.

"I'll tell you, Ben. Strange as it seems, I'm sittin' here lookin' up at that cliff feeling like hell — but I'm thinking about that dog of mine. Damn if I don't miss her."

"It's some time since she disappeared," Cantwell said.

"I'll tell you something else, Ben. I've always thought Dallas did away with her."

"Dallas? Why'd he do that? It'd be senseless . . . we all liked that dog."

"Just a feelin'," Benedict said.

"Indians more'n likely," Cantwell said. "Sneaked up and speared her when she started barkin' — or she just ran off and got lost."

"She never went far from the wagons or the animals," Benedict said wearily. "Back home, back in Sangamon County, when she was a pup I kept her tied. Afterward she was never one to go far. Some dogs are like that, you know, especially females."

"Dallas's got some mean ways," Cantwell said. "I guess we've all seen him belt that slave around for no particular reason."

"Got attached to that dog," Benedict said. "Guess I'm getting old . . . had three daughters and they grew up and married one by one, the last girl shortly after my wife died. Came the night when there was just me and old John Blue and that dog. It was about then that I started thinking about moving west."

Cantwell nodded his head up and down, his lips pursed. Maybe Dallas had lured the dog away and killed her just to hurt Benedict. There were deep currents in Mecom's nature that made him unpredictable. But the damn dog didn't mean anything now. Things were going to change . . . the party had picked Benedict to lead them because he was like them, a plain, ordinary farmer. And they respected him. But when they saw that pulling their guts up the mountain had been for nothing, they'd choose a new captain, sure as hell they would. In years to come, in California, it'd be worth a lot to a man to have led a party over the sierra. The Cantwell Party . . .

16

THREE AXES NOW, filed and whetstoned, cutting wider, cutting deeper, past the shaggy, spongy bark, through the sapwood, into the heartwood. Three axes, hitting the wood, the sound insistent, joining with the echoes, building up, a relentless sound that shattered the quiet of the glade.

Dallas Mecom chopped with a methodical savage rhythm, his long yellow hair loose, his shirt soaked with sweat. Facing him, Joseph, his slave, was slowing down but he still worked with quiet resolve, swinging the axe easily, his eyes never leaving the cut. And now Van Sciber, holding his axe too short, flailing at a small cut of his own, swinging too hard with scant effect.

Dallas stopped, leaving his axe in the wood and one by one the others did the same, stepping back from the tree, appraising their work.

"Where's Silvera?"

"Down around his wagon," Van Sciber said. "Fiddlin' around with that stallion." He was tired, he wanted to rest, sleep, but there wasn't anything that'd make him quit now.

"It ain't like he's really one of us," Dallas said, rubbing the back of his sweaty neck, "but I figger he oughta help."

"You're right," Van Sciber said. "Three of us doing all the work."

He thought of their meeting the Silveras. A light wagon pulled by four mules. A man and his wife. A girl about Naomi's age. They had come north from Santa Fe to sell a string of horses. They didn't want to return because of the war but Dallas hadn't wanted them to join the party, said the others had no right to allow them without his say-so. He didn't like Spaniards, never had, never would, and now that war had started down in Texas, they were the enemy . . .

But Ben Cantwell had won Dallas over. He'd convinced Dallas that Silvera would be a valuable addition to the small party. War could end before they got to California — everybody knew that — but just in case it wasn't over, it was best they had a real Spaniard with them. Someone who really knew the lingo. A friend.

"Where's Billy?" he asked Dallas.

"He went off looking for Cheatham."

Van Sciber looked upward at the awesome pillar of living wood, at the lowest of the branches, thicker than most ordinary trees would ever grow, gnarled and twisted with age. The biggest tree in America and they'd found it.

He was tired but the chopping had been good for him;

his body ached and he was hungry but he'd sleep tonight, sleep without dreaming.

An hour later Oskar Mittenthaler walked up the rise toward the tree. The extra wagon tongue he carried, tied to the bed of his wagon, had come loose and he'd finally secured it.

He went to John Van Sciber.

"You must stop this."

Dallas left his axe stuck in the cut and stood frowning at him.

"We just started, Oskar."

Mittenthaler ignored him. Dallas was trash. It didn't seem possible that John Van Sciber would associate with anyone like Dallas, let alone join him in the destruction of something so magnificent.

"Come," he said.

"Leave him be," Dallas shouted. "Man wants to chop. Can't you see that?"

"This is not good," Mittenthaler said to Van Sciber. "This chopping . . . you, a man such as you . . ."

"You should help us, Oskar," Van Sciber said.

"It's a bad thing," Mittenthaler said. "Nothing good will come from it."

Dallas stepped toward him.

"He's stayin' here. He's choppin'."

Van Sciber stared at him. There was a sudden savage look about Dallas that he'd never seen — in another moment he'd be at Mittenthaler's throat.

"No," he said. "I'm finished."

"Stay," Dallas said. It was a command.

Van Sciber shook his head. Dallas had pushed him too far.

"I'll rest for an hour."

He stood and waited until Dallas turned and began chopping. Then, with Oskar Mittenthaler, he went down the slope to find his wife.

"I'm still hungry," Billy Black said. "Wish to hell we had more meat."

He had returned to the tree and sat tossing twigs and pieces of bark into the fire. The others were silent. Jones lay close to him, eyes closed, hands folded over his greasy buckskins. Manuel Silvera lay with his head against one of the logs they'd dragged down the slope to burn, staring at Dallas and his slave swinging their axes at the tree.

He threw another twig into the fire. Every last scrap of meat was gone but he was hungrier now than he'd been before. They'd roasted the butchered deer and eaten it, all of them except Lydia Hassler.

Jones did the cutting, holding out piece after piece on the point of his knife, dividing it among the party — Oskar and Anna Mittenthaler, John Blue, Gideon Hassler, Manuel Silvera and his wife and daughter, John Van Sciber, Betty Van Sciber, Joseph, each of them taking their small share.

"There's meat if you want it," Jones said. He spoke without raising his head or opening his eyes.

"Where?" Billy asked.

"Benedict's cow."

"Damn," Billy said. "Don't say that." The idea frightened him. Benedict had started with four fine black-and-white cows. It'd be a sin to slaughter the last one left.

"Mittenthaler's got an ox on its last legs," Jones said.

"You're talkin' crazy."

"It's a fact, boy," Jones said. "That animal's about to keel over."

It was, Billy knew, half-true anyway. All the oxen were lame and footsore and half-dead from the desert crossing but Mittenthaler had one that was thinner than any of them and seemed to be half-blind or crazy in the head from too much sun or bad water.

"The animal is still strong," Silvera said.

"Mittenthaler'll never get that wagon over this mountain," Jones said. "Not with them two animals and one of them half-dead."

Dallas dropped his axe and walked toward them.

"You seen Van Sciber?"

"He's sleepin'. In his wagon."

"He was choppin'," Dallas said. "Then Mittenthaler came up here and he quit on me."

"He's tired," Billy said. "He's old, remember that, and he ain't used to hard work — but he'll be back."

"You ever chop much?"

"Chop? Sure I did. Plenty."

Dallas didn't say anything.

"Cordwood," Billy said. "Me and Lee. We used to hire out . . ."

Dallas turned away, smiling as if he didn't believe it.

Billy looked away, into the fire, feeling anger rise up in him. *Damn you, Dallas, you ain't the only sonofabitch can swing an axe . . .*

"I was wondering," Dallas said, "if you was goin' to take a crack at it."

"Guess I will," Billy said without looking up. "Before we go."

Dallas shrugged. "Maybe you better not. Maybe Cheatham wouldn't like it. He don't favor what we're doin'."

"That don't matter," Billy said. "Nobody tells me what I can't do."

"He's still hungry, Dallas," Jones said without moving a muscle or opening his eyes. "I was tellin' him how Mittenthaler's ox was on its last legs . . . man can't work on an empty belly."

"Maybe Lee'll come back with another deer," Billy said. He didn't like Jones talking about killing the ox.

Dallas sat down on the ground and then stretched out flat on his back.

"Time I had some rest," he said. "But I tell you — this choppin' makes a man feel like a man."

Billy stood up. He looked at Dallas and then walked around the fire to the tree. Dallas's axe was there, lying among the pine needles and the fresh chips and he reached down and picked it up and moved opposite Joseph and began to cut into the tree.

Behind the others, almost unnoticed and totally ignored, John Blue sat, still gnawing on a scrap of meat. The tree had stood since time began. It was an ancient thing, not to be disturbed, but now the Whites were here as they were everywhere with their fire and sharp tools. The day was dying. Soon the sun would go. The dark of the night would pass over them.

He shivered. Long ago when he was a tiny child the first Whites came to his village as darkness turned to dawn, shooting their guns, killing men and women and children and even dogs, chasing the frightened horses, shouting and screaming as they burned everything that would burn, smashing all else, even his tiny playthings . . .

He was suddenly chilled and, buttoning up his tattered black coat, he got up and hurried to his wagon.

17

"Look at that," Benedict said.

Cantwell swore under his breath. The ridge had broken and pushed outward, creating a narrow path upward, steep and rock filled and blocked with small, twisted trees; but it could be cleared and, using several yoke of oxen, the wagons, one at a time, could be pulled up. Benedict now would lead them to California.

"I've got a feeling we'll make it now," Benedict said. "Straight over the sierra to the Promised Land." He was happy. He thought of Theodosia Grant.

They tied their horses and made their way up the steep slope, picking their way around boulders and stunted trees, up the steep grade to the top of the ridge. Ahead, the pine-covered slope offered no obstacles.

"It'll be a hard pull up," Cantwell said. "Hell of a job clearing that path."

"I'll send some of them ahead to clear the way," Benedict said. "Billy and Lee. Joseph. Jamie Mecom."

He studied the sky. "Snow. That's the real danger."

"Jones isn't worried."

"Jones's never been this far west. Never been in these mountains," Benedict said. "And I wouldn't trust his word either. From what I've read and from what Bentley told me back at the river we're about due for it. Look at that sky."

Cantwell shrugged. He'd take Jones's word.

"Let's get back to Jamie," Benedict said. "Tell him the good news."

When they reached Jamie they'd expected to find the wagons in sight. They walked to the edge of a slab of granite which gave them a commanding view of the long, gentle, tree-covered slope below. Somewhere down there, Benedict knew, John Blue was urging his oxen on, straining upward. Something about the camp had upset the old Indian and he would be happy to leave it.

"Coffee's ready," Jamie said.

"Where in hell are they?" Cantwell asked.

They walked back to the fire and sat down. Another hour, Benedict reasoned; if they didn't come in the next hour he'd ride down and find them.

"Go and sleep," Cantwell said to him, as Jamie poured the boiling coffee into their tin cups. "You found a way over that ridge and you've had a good meal. Stop worrying. Just curl up and sleep and before you get your eyes closed they'll be here."

Benedict blew on his coffee. The day was ending; the mountain was already cold and the birds and the tiny ground squirrels had stopped their chatter. Cantwell was right. Since they started up the mountain he'd been worrying too much. A leader should learn to take care of himself, eat and rest to be ready for the bad times.

"Something coming," Jamie said.

"Damn good ears," Cantwell said. They stood up and walked to the rise.

"It's Webster," Jamie said.

"The wagons'll be behind him," Benedict said, but there was an urgency in the movement of the horse and rider that disturbed him. A flood of images flashed through his mind: one of the Grant boys could have fallen under the wagon; someone could have been killed or wounded by the accidental firing of a pistol; Indians could have run off the stock or killed some of them.

"I can't see any wagons," Cantwell said.

Benedict took off his hat and reworked the old crease in it. He brushed back his hair and put the hat on again. The wagons had to be down there, slowly pulling up the slope. They just had to be.

Five minutes later Webster Shaughnessey, pale and sweaty from exertion, reached them, his horse quivering from fatigue, blowing little clouds of steam in the cold air.

"They're not coming," he said.

"What in hell's happened now?" Cantwell almost shouted.

Webster slid off his horse. He removed his eyeglasses,

75

wiped them clean with a handkerchief. He went to the fire. Cantwell handed him a cup of steaming coffee and he began to tell them about the accidental death of Gideon Hassler's son, the morning burial by the big rock, and the refusal of Dallas to move up the mountain.

"Is it just Dallas?" Cantwell broke in.

Webster shook his head and watched Jamie lead his horse away, wondering how two brothers could be so different.

"Van Sciber too. Said he wanted to rest. And Billy Black."

"Lee?" Benedict asked.

"He was off hunting."

"Damn his hunting . . . what did Mittenthaler say?"

"He wanted to move out. Mrs. Grant wanted to leave. And the Silveras — but I thought it best not to break up the party. You always said . . ."

"You were right," Benedict said. "You did the right thing."

Webster blew on the hot coffee and sipped it.

"Jones?" Cantwell asked. "Where was Jones?"

"With Dallas."

"Damn his stinking hide," Cantwell said. "I turn my horse over to him and it's twice now he's gone against us."

"Let's get back there as soon as we can," Benedict said.

"Day's going to end before we can do it," Cantwell said, looking at the brooding sky.

Benedict poured the rest of his coffee on the fire and it hissed and began to smoke and die.

"We'll just have to keep moving until we get there."

18

NIGHT FOLLOWED the black shadows down the mountain, bringing a chilling breeze; Manuel Silvera spilled an arm-load of wood on the fire, sending the flames high, lighting the area around the tree, causing the shadows to loom large and spectral.

Oskar Mittenthaler came up the slope and watched the men chopping the tree. Dallas and his black man were swinging their axes with new-found ferocity; they worked in unison, as a team, widening the cut that Dallas had started in the morning.

John Van Sciber had returned. He stood apart from Dallas and Joseph and worked on his own cut, swinging an axe that had never been used before, a new light axe that he swung with little skill.

Billy Black had joined them and he worked now on a cut of his own, standing with his broad muscular back to the others, swinging his axe, intoxicated with the act of destruction.

Lee Cheatham had drunk too much from Van Sciber's jug of whiskey and had a violent argument with Billy Black about the chopping. He sat now, staring at the flames, withdrawn and sullen, half-asleep.

Mittenthaler went to the fire and stood close to Manuel Silvera. He'd seen things like this before . . . mindless assaults on the good, on the magnificent. There was an urge to destroy as well as to build; an impulse to smash and obliterate that was hidden just under the surface. And now it had come to them.

"Don't you chop, Manuel?"

The other man stared at him, then at the choppers and back at him again. "It is . . . how you say . . . a thing a child would do."

"A bad child."

"Yes . . . *malo.*"

They moved a few inches closer to the fire and held out their hands to feel the warmth of the flames.

"Will we leave tomorrow?" Silvera asked.

"I will leave tomorrow."

"I go with you."

When the chill left him Oskar Mittenthaler went down the darkened slope to Gideon Hassler's wagon. He stood just within the pale of light cast by their small fire. The preacher sat with his wife, staring into the flames. Mittenthaler stepped closer.

"I do not wish to . . . intrude," he said.

Gideon turned his head but said nothing.

"Come," Lydia Hassler said, "join us."

"It's a bad time to come," Mittenthaler said.

"A good time," Lydia said.

"Your boy . . . Lucas . . . if there was anything I could say except that —"

"I understand."

"I am very sorry."

"Thank you."

Gideon Hassler stood up. "Thank you, Oskar."

"I came to ask something," Mittenthaler said.

"The tree?" Hassler said.

Oskar nodded. "You must go up there and stop them."

Gideon dropped his eyes and looked at the fire.

"It is a bad time for you," Mittenthaler said, "but you are the only one. They'll listen to you. A man of God."

"Why do they do it?" Lydia said wearily.

Gideon looked up toward the sound of axes.

"We can't let them do it," Mittenthaler said. "It is — a godlike thing."

He stepped closer to the preacher. There was suddenly an empty, hollow feeling in his chest. Long ago in the old country he'd had the same exact sense of fear, of dread. He and the other boys had circled the lone cow they had found high on a mountain meadow . . .

"Stop them," he said. "Stop them before it's too late."

Gideon nodded. Foreigners seemed to make a fuss about trees and land. But Oskar was a sensible man and he was right — the attack on the tree was out of control.

"We could have died in the desert," Lydia said. "Now those men are acting like a pack of fools, wasting their strength. Go, Gideon. Tell them to stop. They'll listen to you."

"I'll go," Gideon said. He stood up. Benedict and Cantwell were gone. And Webster Shaughnessey. The sensible ones. The others were drinking, throwing themselves at the tree like madmen. The party was falling apart and it was time he talked to them, brought them to their senses.

"I'll stay down here," Mittenthaler said. "By my own wagon."

Gideon nodded, buttoning his coat, smoothing out the wrinkles. It was best that Oskar stayed out of it. He was a foreigner and Dallas Mecom didn't like him.

"Thank you, Mrs. Hassler," Oskar Mittenthaler said. "I am sorry I had to come . . . you're a . . . very fine lady."

She watched his figure merge with the darkness. *A fine lady*. None of them knew her, not really. She was the preacher's wife and most of them treated her in a high-falutin way when the plain truth was that she'd come out of a family that was lazy, good for nothing, poor as church mice. Gideon, riding past their place on a scorching August day, had first seen her standing barefooted in the mud pouring slop for the hogs. But that was a faint memory; now she could read and write and cook properly, do all the things that people expected of a preacher's wife.

Gideon Hassler walked up the dark slope and stood just within the circle of light cast by the fire. The men swung their axes in utter concentration, their shadows rippling over the tree, which rose up into the darkness, its bulk defying their dwarfish figures.

Godlike, the German had said. *It's a godlike thing.*

Lee Cheatham stood up slowly and came toward him. "They've gone crazy," he said thickly.

Gideon nodded. "I've come to talk."

Cheatham turned and shouted and the two figures around the fire stirred and sat up. Manuel Silvera and Jones. Lee Cheatham waved to the choppers and one by one they stopped working and came to the fire, Dallas Mecom and Joseph, Van Sciber and Billy Black.

"Reverend wants to talk to us," Lee shouted. He stepped away, almost falling, and Gideon Hassler looked around at the faces close to him, faces moving closer, defensive and hostile.

"This chopping, this cutting. You must stop."

They stood, staring at him, as if they were deaf, as if they hadn't heard or understood.

"This tree," he said louder. "It's a special thing. Can't you see. Something we must not mutilate. It's a thing of God."

There was only silence. He stared at them, into each rigid face, into each feral eye. The fire snapped on the wood and the glow of it turned their faces red. They were alien men now and they hated him, for he'd touched something deep within them. Outside the ring of fire the night was pitch black, and he was afraid.

Van Sciber came toward him. "We thought you came to help."

"Tree killed your boy," Billy said.

"Help us," Van Sciber said. "You've got every reason to be with us on this."

They were closer now, ringing him in a half-circle, smelling of sweat and whiskey. Dallas reached out and seized his wrist and he winced from the pain.

"You need a drink," Dallas said, and put the jug in his hand.

"Don't you make trouble now," Jones said softly. "I got a bellyful of people tellin' me what I can't do, what I can do. First Benedict, and now . . ."

"Drink," Dallas said.

He lifted the jug, swallowed a mouthful of whiskey, felt it burn his throat.

"Little Lucas," Billy Black said. "He'd want you to chop, want you to help us."

"Mittenthaler," Dallas said. "He put you up to this, didn't he?"

"He said it was . . . godlike," Gideon said.

"That don't make no sense," Billy said.

"Blasphemy," Van Sciber said. "Only God is godlike. Isn't that right?"

"Yes," Gideon said quickly. "That's right. Only God is godlike . . . cut the tree . . ."

They turned away from him and moved closer to the fire, passing the jug from one to another. Gideon followed them. The fear was gone. He was linked to them now in secret shame. He was safe. They would never humiliate him. The Lord and the Book were far away across the deserts and plains and unnamed rivers. Here, in the stark black night of the mountain there was only Dallas Mecom.

"Let's git that ox," Jones said softly.

They turned from the parson and stared at the Mountain Man, knowing they would do it, knowing that they would take the animal and slaughter it. Nothing would stop them.

"It's Mittenthaler's," Cheatham said quietly. The whiskey had made him drowsy but he was suddenly alert. And afraid. They were going to kill. And it seemed natural that they'd kill something now; the savage attack on the tree was only part of something that was all around them, something as black as the night, that made his heart beat louder, made his hands tremble.

"Damn him," Billy Black shouted.

"You can't take a man's ox," Lee said. "It's his property . . . it's stealin'."

"He's right," Jones said. "We can't take it."

The others stared at him.

"We'll have to buy that animal," Jones said, nodding his head. He smiled and they saw his long yellow teeth. Then something glinted before him — his knife held point up in his gnarled, clawlike hand.

"What's the parson say?" Billy Black shouted.

Dallas stepped toward Gideon. "That animal's on his last legs, Reverend," he said quickly.

"Take it," Gideon said. "Slaughter it. It'll die anyway, die on the mountain . . ."

He felt dizzy. The whiskey burned his throat. Blood pounded in his brain. He felt drained and hollow;

he went closer to the fire and sat down on a log, staring at the flames, rubbing his wrist.

"God-*damn*," Dallas shouted. "It's the best night we've had since Independence."

"You're crazy," Cheatham said. "You can't just up and take a man's ox — how's Mittenthaler goin' to pull that wagon?"

"You gonna stop me?" Dallas said, pushing past him.

"We'll fix a spit," Van Sciber said. "I've got an iron in my wagon. Somebody give me a hand."

"I'll go," Manuel Silvera said. There was his wife and his daughter. If he didn't help, they might not give a share of the meat — he'd help the Americans and keep his mouth shut. Mecom was running things now; it was dangerous to anger him.

"Let's you and me get that critter," Dallas said to Jones. "Rest of you get wood."

They went into the darkness. The others scattered to find firewood. Cheatham stood looking at Gideon Hassler who sat like a ragged scarecrow staring into the flames.

Hassler turned, started to speak, then dropped his eyes.

"What the hell kind of a man are you?" Cheatham asked.

Hassler stared into the fire.

"You could've stopped them," Cheatham said.

Hassler shook his head back and forth, his thin, corded neck and lined face, red now from the glow of the fire. Cheatham was young. He didn't understand.

"No," he said. "Not here, not now . . ."

❋

Dallas led the frightened ox up the dark slippery slope, pulling and tugging on a length of rope that he'd tied to one of the beast's horns; it balked and fought, bracing its hooves against the slope, twisting its head to fight the rope, its large eyes rolling, bellowing and snorting as if it already understood its fate. And Jones was behind, pulling its tail, sticking his knife into the hindquarters, shouting, cursing . . .

They reached the fire and the others came out of the darkness with heavy armloads of wood. Joseph carried a single log, balanced on his shoulder. Manuel Silvera and Van Sciber came up the long slope with the iron they'd use as a spit.

Dallas left Jones holding the ox, went into the darkness and came back with Cheatham's rifle. Billy Black moved close to him, his rifle ready. John Van Sciber joined them, rubbing the long barrel of his pistol with his left hand.

"Don't do it," Lee Cheatham shouted from the other side of the fire.

"Shut your mouth, boy," Jones said.

Dallas pointed the rifle at the ox's head. Jones dropped the rope and moved away.

"*Stop!*" Lee Cheatham shouted.

Dallas fired, the animal shuddered and in the same instant Billy shot. Van Sciber stepped forward very quickly and fired his pistol twice into the thrashing head.

The air was suddenly bitter with the smell of burning gunpowder and the smell of blood. Jones fell on his knees beside the dead beast, raising his knife, stabbing into the carcass, lost in wild elation . . .

19

WEBSTER SHAUGHNESSEY, moving ahead of the others, worked his way from one half-remembered landmark to another. Now and then he would stop so that Ben Cantwell could move up to hold his horse while he went ahead on foot. It was slow work but not as difficult as they'd imagined. The slope was even and the moon full.

He couldn't rid himself of the memory of Dallas and the others telling him that they weren't moving out. It was open and senseless rebellion. Benedict was their natural leader; a man skilled with animals and wagons and imbued with a sense of purpose. Back at the river when they'd left Bentley and the larger party, they'd chosen him captain. Now, the same men had turned against him. The party had ceased to exist. Dallas and the others had destroyed it by some dark consuming urge to stay at the tree.

"Look," Jamie said. "Their fire."

"Must be a big one," Benedict said. A bolt of worry crossed his mind. Indians — or even Mexicans. The fire was their wagons — Theodosia's.

"Late in the night for one that size," Jamie said. Maybe it was a service, prayers and such, for Lucas Hassler.

"Glad it's big," Cantwell said. "Gives us something to guide on."

"Let's hold up awhile," Benedict said. "Catch our breath."

They stopped in the moonlight, resting with their jaded animals.

"What'll you be doing in California?" Cantwell asked Webster.

Webster shrugged. "I don't really know, Ben. I'd like to see this war end first."

"War's probably over now," Cantwell said. "Hell, them Mexes can't fight. We'll take California and the whole shebang."

"It'll be a bloody war," Webster said. "Polk thinks it'll be over in a few months — but he's wrong."

"It always struck me strange," Cantwell said. "A young rooster like you. Educated and all. You against this war."

"There's plenty against it."

"There's more favorin' it."

"It'll hurt us," Webster said. "We'll win it, sure, but it'll split us, North and South, when they get all this new land and try to figure which is slave, which is free."

"They'll settle it," Cantwell said. "Always have, one way or another."

"I don't know," Webster said. "War's got a way of rilin' up people, stirrin' up things . . . it could split this country right down the middle."

Cantwell fell silent. It didn't set with him that Webster didn't favor Polk and the war; seemed like all Americans should be for the war and against the Mexicans — and if it was anyone but Webster he'd have said it to his face. But Webster was a smart young fellow and there was no telling what would become of him if he played his cards right. When the war was over and California would be American, there'd be no end of opportunities for men like Webster Shaughnessey.

"Let's go," Benedict said. When they got back to the others he'd quit. If they wouldn't follow him they'd follow Dallas. If they were afraid of the mountain they could go back down to the desert.

20

OSKAR MITTENTHALER SAT in the glow of the lantern next to the Grant wagon, staring at his wife and Theodosia as they washed his throbbing head wound. He did not speak nor did they; Anna had at last stopped crying and she moved back now as Theodosia wound a clean piece of cloth around his head.

It was unbelievable. Dallas Mecom and Jones had come to take his poor, rib-thin and footsore ox out of the corral and in the madness of shouting and struggling that followed, he had been knocked unconscious, probably by Jones's rifle.

He remembered coming to, lying on the ground in the corral, a wet rag on his throbbing forehead, looking up at his wife and Inez Silvera in the yellow glare of a lantern, then being helped up and along by Theodosia Grant and John Blue.

"They took the ox," he said.

He closed his eyes. Benedict must be coming back. They must warn him. He didn't understand about the tree and what it had done to Dallas and Jones, to Billy Black and even John Van Sciber. Benedict wouldn't know that he was in great danger, that the party was forever split, that they had to flee from the tree . . .

"They're crazy," Anna said. She turned to Theodosia. "They could have killed him. That Jones . . . he's an animal."

"Mecom," Oskar said without opening his eyes. "Wants to destroy everything . . . it will get worse. We must leave, Anna, in the morning. Soon as possible."

"Mr. Benedict," Anna said. "He should never have left . . ."

Theodosia suddenly thought of Naomi and hurried to the front of the wagon and called out. But she knew there'd be no answer. She knew where the girl would be.

She turned from the Mittenthalers and ran into the darkness, up the slope toward the tree and the great fire that roared before it. She tripped and fell, hurting her left hand. She began to cry, thinking of her husband. *I should have turned back when you died, Bill — now, it's too late, too late* . . .

She got up, stumbled on, seeing Naomi drawn to the fire like some fragile moth to a bright light. And then she was near the fire and saw men standing and crouching around it, drinking, shouting at each other, watching the slow turn of the spit; beyond them someone stripped to the waist chopped at the great raw wound in the tree.

Naomi stood in the darkness close to one of the trees,

outside of the pale light thrown by the fire. Leaning against the tree, his face close to hers, was Billy Black, drunk and bare-chested, his long hair hanging wildly over his face.

Theodosia hurried forward seizing the girl's wrist. *"What are you doing here?"*

Naomi pulled away. "I came to . . . see. I want to see."

"How long have you been here?"

"She jus' come, Miz Grant," said Billy Black. "She jus' come up to see."

"How could you?" Theodosia asked. "You almost cried when they started to cut it. Now . . ."

"I want to see," Naomi said. Her face was flushed and her eyes extra bright as if they were feverish or filled with tears.

"You can't stay here," Theodosia said quietly. "We must go back to the wagon. Do you understand, Naomi? You must come back and help me."

"I want to stay," Naomi said.

"We're going."

"No."

Dallas Mecom was behind her, brushing back his blond hair, wiping both his hands on his pants.

"Evenin', Mrs. Grant, Miss Naomi," he said. "Fun's about to start." He reached for Theodosia but she moved backward.

"Don't touch me, Mr. Mecom."

Dallas laughed. "Don't pay to be distant, Mrs. Grant. Things change, I've learned."

"We're leaving," Theodosia said.

"You stay with me," Billy Black said to Naomi.

"There'll be meat soon," Dallas said. They were scared of him and that was good.

Theodosia reached for Naomi, took her arm, and started down the slope. Then she slipped. Dallas lunged forward, catching her around the waist. She cried out, feeling the wild power of his arms, the smell of whiskey, the man smell.

"Let me go . . ."

"Just helpin' out," Dallas said, and she was free, running, pulling the girl behind her, his laughter following her through the darkness.

Betty Van Sciber awoke, trembling and sweaty hot, trying to force the fragments of the dream out of her mind. They were in the desert again with the horizon shimmering around them and the wagons moving abreast of each other to escape the alkali dust which caked on their faces, making ghoulish masks.

The emigrant guidebook said two days for a crossing but they took six, traveling with almost no stops, almost dying of thirst, leaving dead horses and oxen in their rutted wake. The first to falter was one of Mr. Benedict's two remaining cows. It began to stagger and lose its way and then slumped down; all the prodding and kicking by John Blue had no effect. They rolled on until it was only a black speck far behind them in the white nothingness.

The sun sucked the moisture from the wooden wagons. Spokes dried out and rattled in their loose sockets, iron rims worked loose from their wheels and fell off, the hubs cried for grease, screeching like lost souls.

The desert was the final blow. It sweated away their reserve, made them lightheaded and irrational. On the second night, Dallas Mecom and Lee Cheatham began a minor argument and within minutes they stood pointing guns, ready to kill each other over some trifle. And, on the last day, near a scummy waterhole she'd heard the whirring of a rattlesnake and began screaming and could not stop even when Joseph came running and killed it . . .

She lay now, studying the changing patterns of light and shadow that danced on the patched and faded whitetop above her; ghostly images created by the roaring fire that the men had built close to the tree.

She'd tried to read by candlelight, but the tensions of the day had been too much with her: the discovery of the tree, the death of Lucas Hassler, the chopping, the beating of Oskar Mittenthaler, the killing of his ox. Then, at last, she'd fallen asleep but only to dream again, a new dream that repelled her. She groaned now, pressing the palm of each hand over both eyes. She began to weep.

Dear God, what am I doing here? But she knew. It had been her own choice. She'd married John Van Sciber to escape the rabble of small children she'd struggled to teach; she married to flee the narrowness of her life, to move, to travel, to get away, anywhere.

Now, the premonitions of disaster that had haunted her early in the journey had burst into open fear. They were, all of them, weakened by the needless stupid-

93

ities and mistakes of the long trip. The enforced companionship and unspoken fear had rubbed nerves raw, breeding distrust and hate. Their unity was gone, eroded from a hundred minor arguments, weakened by jealousy and hardship. And now some elemental lust to hurt and destroy had at last broken through the thin layer of civilized behavior. She thought of a familiar scene: two small boys standing toe to toe in the dusty schoolyard, smashing their fists into each other's faces.

Now she felt herself falling asleep and she fought the recurrent dream that shamed her: Dallas Mecom holding her, blond hair spilling over his face, his hands hard on her shoulders . . .

Jones edged away from the fire and stood in the dark for several minutes watching the others. Then, walking slowly in case someone was watching, he went down the slope, following the shadows, circling around the line of wagons to the depression where the oxen had been gathered and the horses picketed. He found the opening of the corral and made his way quietly toward the animals. Silvera was supposed to be there on guard but he was at the fire, stuffing himself with roasted meat, drinking whiskey, chopping at the tree.

But there was someone among the animals. He crept closer, knife ready. They hadn't seen Indians or any sign of them this side of the desert but you had to figure they were around waiting to slip in and run off horses or oxen. Now, moving closer, he saw Nilda Silvera, standing in a shaft of moonlight, with the stallion and the mules, feeding them — cut grass most likely — from her cupped hands, speaking softly to them in Spanish.

He moved forward. He'd take her too, a nice little Mex girl to keep him company. Konk her on the head with the handle of his knife, tie her over the horse and light out same as he'd planned. There'd be a stink when they found her gone, along with the two horses, but none of them except Silvera would try followin' him to get her back — not like it was that pretty little Naomi or Van Sciber's yellow-haired woman. They'd talk it up but none of them would risk it.

Suddenly, as if knowing his thoughts, the girl turned and stared into the darkness, not toward him but behind her. Then she was gone, running light-footed up the slope, slipping under the ropes that had been strung around the top of the depression, hurrying toward her wagon, the whitetop aglow from a candle or lamp.

Jones swore softly. No chance of gettin' her now. Whatever had spooked her had changed her life more'n she'd ever know.

He walked forward to where the girl had stood. Cantwell's appaloosa was there and Silvera's prized stallion. The Spaniard had forgotten to take it out of the corral, tie it to the tailgate of his wagon as he did each evening. He spoke to them, made the familiar sounds they knew. He'd take the stallion.

Then suddenly he spun around, bending low, the knife before him, eyes straining to pierce the darkness. There was someone close to him.

It was John Blue, sitting on the ground with his back

against a tree not twelve feet away. Moonlight shown on his ancient, withered face: he stared straight ahead without moving, without recognition, as if his mind was far away, sitting as still as a man frozen or dead.

But he wasn't dead, Jones knew. And he had been there all along, watching him come, watching him as he'd moved closer to the Mex girl, staring at him now without fear as he crouched low, the knife glinting. *Benedict's goddamn Indian.*

He leaped forward and drove the knife into the old man's throat, then thrust again and again as the body crumpled and slid sideways to the ground. And turning he ran to the picket line, slashed the rope that held the big stallion and led it up and out of the corral, down the mountain into the darkness.

Inez Silvera opened her eyes and saw her daughter in the flickering light of the candle; in a half-dream she'd walked through a field of new green corn with the sun hot on her face, the soil soft and cool on her bare feet.

"Where's Father?" the girl said. She sat with her knees drawn up, staring at the primal blackness beyond the half-opened flaps at the back of the wagon.

Her mother turned her face away from the light. "With the others."

"Why does he cut the tree?"

Inez closed her eyes. Her dream had been pleasant but it was forever gone. Now there was only the sound of the axes.

"I'm afraid," the girl said. "I went to say good-night

to the mules and down there in the darkness was . . .
something frightened me."

"Blow out the candle. Sleep."

"Why do they cut the tree?"

Inez opened her eyes. She'd knelt alone in the cool
darkness between the high kneelike roots of the tree. If
the men had not spoiled it, she would have placed a statue
of the Virgin there, made a shrine.

"Because they are men."

"What do you mean?"

"They prove themselves," Inez said. "On the tree. Man
against man. It's great and tall and old. They want to
see it fall."

"I don't understand."

"It's like a beautiful woman. All men want her. To
prove themselves. To show other men that they are men."

Nilda pulled the blanket around her. In the new place
her father would have a herd of mares and they would
breed fine horses to sell to the Americans who were, year
after year, moving west over the mountain. She would
wear fine clothes. She would be beautiful. Young men
would come to buy horses. She would become the wife
of a great landowner, live in a fine thick-walled house
with servants to cook and serve her.

"Did you say your prayers?" Inez asked.

"I forgot."

"Blow out the candle and pray."

The girl bent over the flame and blew and it was pitch
black. Inez thought of the three men up ahead on the
mountain waiting for them. The party should have gone

on as soon as the boy was buried. Now the men had killed an ox. And in the tree they had found something to hate, something noble to destroy. They had said things to Manuel that had made him sullen and short-tempered and he'd come to the wagon, smelling of American whiskey, taken his axe, and without a word to her gone to the tree.

21

"It's Benedict."

The chopping halted. The men standing and squatting around the fire got up and walked slowly toward the dark figures of Benedict, Cantwell, Shaughnessey, and Jamie Mecom slumped forward on their saddles. The only sound came from the fire as the dry wood snapped, as the flames roared.

"What in hell is goin' on here?" Benedict said quietly. He looked at the half-devoured carcass of the ox, at the mutilated tree, at the faces of the men.

No one answered him. He swung down off his horse and limped slowly to the fire. None of it seemed real. The huge fire whipped by the wind. The terrible thing they'd done to the tree. The animal look on their faces.

"Are the Hasslers here?"

Gideon Hassler came out of the shadows, tall, bent over, woebegone. He smelled of whiskey.

"I'm sorry," Benedict said. "Webster told me about Lucas. I'm real sorry . . ."

He reached out and held Gideon's thin, bony shoulder, then grasped his hand, felt the man shaking.

"It was a bad night all around," Benedict said. "But it's about over. Why don't you go get some sleep."

"Yes," Gideon said quietly. "I'm tired."

Benedict turned to John Van Sciber.

"What are you doing to the tree?"

The other man brushed back his white hair, started to say something, then dropped his eyes. Benedict moved closer, looking at the other faces around him, sweaty and taut, flushed from whiskey, from the heat of the fire.

"*What are you doing to the tree?*"

"Jus' cuttin' it some," Billy Black said thickly. "We don't know — just messin' with it."

"You've ruined it," Webster shouted from his horse. "Grown men doing a thing like that . . ."

"We'll do what we damn well please," Billy shouted.

"We're going to cut it down," Van Sciber said quietly. "It's the biggest tree there is and we're going to be the ones who did it."

Benedict studied his strange blue eyes.

"Cut it down?" he said. "You must be crazy — even if it was a fittin' thing there's no time."

"We'll make time," Van Sciber said.

"Who killed the ox?" Benedict asked.

"I did," Dallas said.

"They took it from Oskar Mittenthaler," Lee Cheatham said. "And they beat him. Dallas and Jones."

"*Beat* him?" Benedict said. He felt an old fear rise within him. Jones wasn't with them. "Why didn't some of you stop it?"

No one spoke.

"Where's Mittenthaler now?"

"In his wagon," Betty Van Sciber said.

"Where the hell is Jones?"

"He's around somewhere," Billy Black said.

Benedict turned to Dallas. "You kill Mittenthaler's ox?"

"Goddamn, Benedict. You know that animal. It was ready to keel over and die — we figured to put it out of its misery."

The party was forever shattered, Benedict knew. The fire and the hard predatory faces — they were all stirred up and before it was over there'd be hell to pay.

Now, he and Dallas were mortal enemies; they could no longer stay together. One of them would kill the other. His only choice was to move out as quickly as possible. He had to get Theodosia and her boys and Naomi and the Hasslers away from the tree and hope to God that the rest of the party would fight free of Dallas and join him.

He'd come back down the mountain to quit. To turn the leadership over to someone else. But it had all changed. Now there was no leader.

"Take one of his animals," Webster said from his horse. "That'd be the just thing to do."

Damn you Webster, Benedict thought, let me handle this.

Dallas was smiling. "Any man here touches my oxen gets himself shot dead."

"That's hangin' talk," Cantwell said.

Dallas nodded to himself and looked around at the others.

"Damn if that ain't an idea. Maybe that's what this party needs — a hanging."

It was quiet. The hard dry sticks in the fire snapped like pistol shots and the tired horses stamped on the raw earth but no man spoke.

Nilda Silvera ran into the light, crying, moaning, shouting words only a few of them understood, running to her father, hugging him.

"What the hell's wrong now?" Cantwell shouted.

Manuel Silvera held the girl. "Indian dead," he said. "Dead by knife. Stallion gone."

"Diggers," Billy Black shouted.

"Where's Jones?" Cheatham said.

All of them stopped and looked around for the Mountain Man. Jamie Mecom kicked his horse and rode down the slope toward the Grant wagon.

"I saw him leave," Van Sciber said.

"Why'd he kill that miserable Indian?" Dallas shouted.

"Horse," Cheatham said. "He lit out with Silvera's stallion."

"Let's find him," Ben Cantwell said. There was a pistol in his hand, barrel pointed in the air.

If they caught that stinking Mountain Man now, they'd prop up a wagon tongue and hang him, a horse thief, a murderer.

Billy Black grabbed a brand from the fire.

"Let's get him," he shouted, and ran down the hill toward the wagons, toward the depression where the animals were. Jones wasn't one of them now, he was like an enemy soldier.

Inez Silvera stood next to the horse that Manuel had mounted, holding the edge of the saddle.

"Don't leave — I beg you."

"No man steals my stallion."

"You'll never find him. If you do he'll kill you . . . he's a savage, not a man."

"Then I shall become a savage."

"Don't leave us, Manuel."

"I must get my stallion."

"In California we can buy another."

"I must go," Manuel said. He kicked the horse forward and his wife stepped aside and watched him move away toward the darkness.

Benedict was suddenly alone, thinking of John Blue, staring at the torches moving away in the darkness. The old man had suffered from the cold. Only a few days ago, they had talked around the supper fire of the new land where there was never snow or bitter winds.

Jones was miles away now, a greasy brown snake slithering down the mountain. The men were wasting their time. They'd never find him. It was best they didn't.

Theodosia Grant came into the light.

"I'm glad you came back," she said.

"Yes," Benedict said. "So'm I."

When they got to California he would marry Theodosia Grant. He had never spoken to her about it and never would until they were out of the mountains.

"I'm afraid," she said. "Why did he do it — such an old harmless man."

"He was with me all of my life," Benedict said. "My folks took him in when he was a small boy. Maybe five years old. His whole village was wiped out. All but him. Bunch of men rode in looking for some missing cattle. My uncle was with them. Next thing it was a massacre. Nobody ever knew why it happened. Whole settlement destroyed, lock, stock and barrel."

"If he'd only asked for a horse," Theodosia said, "we might have been able to spare one."

"The party's split," he said. "We've got to move on at dawn."

"It's not your fault," she said. "God Himself couldn't have stopped them. They've got some idea they've got to cut down the tree. It's some kind of wildness. Something coming out in them. They were at it all day. This is the first time they've stopped. Hour after hour . . ."

"Dallas started it?"

"Yes. Then he made Joseph work. After that the others joined. Van Sciber. Billy. Most of them, I think. Maybe you can get them to stop . . ."

"No," he said. "It's too late. The rest of us — whoever wants to go — will leave soon as it gets light."

"They'll all come," she said, "now that Jones has gone, now that John Blue . . ."

Benedict shook his head. "They'll stay here, Theodosia."

"Most of them wanted to stay longer at the spring below the mountain, but they followed you, did what you said."

"They won't move now," he said. "This cutting . . . party's up for good."

She said nothing.

"I've got to look after John," he said.

"Yes," she said, "I'll do what I can to help you," and she hurried down the slope beside him, watching the torches moving in the darkness around the wagons, around the corral. Jones frightened her now more than ever. He'd come out of the swirling dust devils that shimmering hot day in the desert and now he'd faded into the black night, out of nowhere, and back to nowhere as if he wasn't a man at all.

Lying in his blankets Jamie Mecom wondered if there'd ever be a time when things would be right again. He'd join the others searching for Jones but he was long gone and it was impossible to try to follow his trail back down the mountain — and they knew Jones would kill anyone who came within range of his rifle.

They'd returned to John Blue, wrapped the body in his robes, and carried him down the slope to the big rock and by torchlight buried him next to Lucas Hassler. Mr. Hassler said a few words over the grave and they'd broken up, each to his own wagon, to try to sleep before the night was totally gone.

Now, without warning, tears welled up in him and he cursed them, wiped them away, and was ashamed. Things were never going to be the same again, never,

never again. It was like something inside of him had popped and broken. Jones had ruined it all. Jones was a murderer and horse thief and renegade and all the time he'd been laughin' up his sleeve at them, waitin' for a chance to get away with a good cut of meat and a prize horse and maybe other things that none of them had missed yet. Jones had been special to him, a real Mountain Man, a real trapper and Indian fighter like the ones he'd read about, living free as a man should, hating cities and towns and even farms but he'd spoiled it all now, spoiled a lot of dreams and plans and wishes . . .

Damn you, Jones, why did you have to do it?

The Mountain

22

BENEDICT AWOKE to the sound of chopping which merged with his dream: Dallas swinging an axe at the tree, which shivered and then slowly began to fall down upon them.

He sat up. Next to him, wrapped in buffalo robes, Webster Shaughnessey and Ben Cantwell stirred and awoke. It was past dawn.

Without speaking they got up and moved stiffly to the remains of the small fire. Webster piled pine sticks on the embers and stirred them and the fire came alive.

"Four wagons," Cantwell said, blowing on his clenched hands. "Mrs. Grant's, Mittenthaler's, Gideon Hassler's, and yours."

Benedict sat the pot in the fire. Last night after they'd buried John Blue, Webster and Ben Cantwell had circulated among the party to determine how many were going.

"It'll have to be three," he said.

Cantwell frowned.

"Mittenthaler lost that yoke in the desert and he's down to one animal so he can't move. But his wagon's good, light and strong. Hassler's is too damn heavy. We'll add his team to Oskar's wagon, scatter his belongings among the rest."

"Hassler might not agree to it," Webster said.

"He's got no choice," Benedict said. "We might end up without any wagons. He's got to agree to it."

"You better tell him," Cantwell said.

"Jamie Mecom's coming," Webster said. "Naomi told me last night."

"Lee and Billy?" Benedict asked.

"Billy won't leave," Webster said. "And Lee's staying with him."

"Damn them," Cantwell said. "Let them stay."

"Did Silvera come back?"

"No."

"Sure hope he didn't catch up with Jones."

Benedict stood up.

"I'm going to see the Hasslers," he said. "You two eat and then get started on the wagons."

He'd eat later. They had to hurry. Theodosia would find something for him once they began moving.

Webster stood up. "I've got to talk to them," he said to Cantwell, nodding toward the choppers. "I'll be back here right away to help."

"They won't listen to you."

"I'll be back, Ben. Make some coffee."

Cantwell shrugged. It didn't matter what time they left as long as they left.

Webster walked up the slope, studying the two men swinging their axes at the raw, V-shaped cut. When he was ten feet away they stopped and looked at him, their faces clouded with distrust.

"What the hell you want, Webster?" Billy Black shouted.

"I came up here to ask you if you're going to break up the party just to chop down a tree."

"It's special," John Van Sciber said. He rubbed his thumb along the edge of the axe blade.

"That's no reason to cut it down."

"It is for us," Van Sciber said.

"Benedict asked you to move out. Why don't you listen to him?"

"Benedict's a farmer," Billy said. "Just a sod buster like the rest of us."

"You elected him captain back at the river," Webster said. "He didn't want it but we all begged him. Now we've got to back him up."

"Most of us want to stay," Van Sciber said. "If anybody's breakin' up the party it's Benedict. We're the majority."

"We ain't goin', Webster," Billy said. "That's that."

Webster shook his head. "Grown men . . . chopping down a tree . . ."

"Hell," Van Sciber said. "Grab an axe. Sooner she goes down sooner we'll all move."

"Not me," Webster said. "I'd be ashamed."

Van Sciber stepped forward, his blue eyes bright with excitement, his face flushed and sweaty from chopping. "Yes, Webster, and when she falls you'll wish you stayed. You'll be sorry. You'll wish you'd had a hand in it . . ."

Webster shook his head and turned away. They'd been caught up in some malevolent urge to destroy. They were trying to kill what they might well worship. He didn't understand and it frightened him.

"Yes," Lydia Hassler said. "We'll do it, Mr. Benedict. If you say it has to be."

She looked sideways at her husband, waiting for him to lift up his head and agree.

Gideon looked up and nodded. "We'll leave the wagon."

Benedict relaxed. He'd talked for ten minutes, explaining why they had to leave their wagon behind, spread their belongings among the others. There were too many wagons, too few men. If they were to make it over the sierra, something would have to be sacrificed.

They understood. He left them and headed for Oskar Mittenthaler. Three wagons now, four women and two children but only five men. Billy Black and Lee Cheatham? Had Webster talked to them? But it was no use begging; if they were coming they'd be on the trail with him.

A pistol shot split the air, he spun around, head low, his heart pounding.

Dallas Mecom was twenty feet from him, a pistol in his hand, pointing skyward.

"You lookin' for me, Benedict?"

"I'm looking for Mittenthaler — why'd you shoot off that pistol?"

The chopping stopped and as the first long minute passed, the rest of the party converged on the two men.

"You come to take my ox," Dallas said, brushing back his long blond hair. "The one you're goin' to give to Mittenthaler."

"I'm leaving, Dallas."

Dallas was smiling. "Back home we had a way of handling cattle thieves."

"No fight," Benedict said. "I'm going over the mountain."

"No guts."

"Call it what you like."

"Goddamn," Billy Black said. "Never thought I'd see Benedict back off, no sir."

"Shut up, Billy," Lee Cheatham shouted. It'd been Webster who'd said something about taking one of Dallas's oxen, not Benedict.

Dallas tossed the pistol aside.

"Your move, Benedict."

Jamie Mecom stepped forward. Dallas had never liked Mr. Benedict. Dallas didn't like being around anybody or anything that made him look second best. But now he'd gone too far. Mr. Benedict would never back down.

"I'm not fighting you," Benedict said quietly. "I told you that. I'm taking my people over the mountain."

Dallas looked around at the others. "Man says he's gonna take my ox, I got a right to fight him."

"We've got all the animals we need," Benedict said.

"You gonna take my ox?" Dallas shouted.

Benedict drew a deep breath and looked at Theodosia, standing behind Jamie Mecom, her face white with strain. "No."

"Never thought I'd see the day," said Billy Black. "Damned if I did."

"Maybe another time," Dallas said. "Maybe in California."

Benedict relaxed. "You'll never see California. None of you. You'll stay and chop at that tree until it's too late."

"We'll cut it down," Van Sciber shouted. "Then over the mountain to California."

Benedict shook his head. "You can't do both, John. No time, no strength for both."

Dallas picked up his pistol. "Long as you're goin', I might as well tell you . . . I killed that dog of yours . . ."

"I figgered that."

"Kicked that damn hound too hard. Figgered I broke his back the way he crawled off draggin' his hind legs . . ."

"Always barked too much," Benedict said. "It was the main thing wrong with her."

"She wasn't barkin'," Dallas said. "I just got sick of lookin' at her."

"I'm glad you told me," Benedict said, and he turned his back on Dallas and walked down the line of wagons to Oskar and Anna Mittenthaler.

Jamie Mecom stared after him. Mr. Benedict turnin' tail instead of fightin' — he was no better than the rest of them, afraid of Dallas, knowin' Dallas was wrong, but scared to fight him.

"I'm not coming," Jamie said to Naomi.

They stood together, near the spring, apart from the wagons yoked and waiting Benedict's word to move.

"Not coming?" She frowned, studied his troubled face.

"I'm stayin' with Dallas."

"Last night you said you'd come," she said. "You promised."

"I *was* goin'," Jamie said, "but I'm stayin' now."

"Why?"

"Dallas said I had to."

"That's a lie, Jamie Mecom. Don't you lie to me."

"It was Mr. Benedict," Jamie said suddenly. "Why didn't he fight? Why didn't he stand up to Dallas?"

"What's that matter?" Naomi said.

"It matters," Jamie said. He bent down and picked up a clublike stick, dry and without bark. "It matters plenty."

"Mr. Benedict's got more sense than fighting your brother."

Jamie hefted the stick, then smashed it against the tree. Girls didn't understand. You had to fight. You always had to even if you knew you'd get whipped.

"You better come," Naomi said. Her eyes were suddenly filled with tears and then she was crying. "You just better come, Jamie . . ."

"Well, I ain't," Jamie said, almost shouting. "I ain't goin' with Mr. Benedict, no sir, not now." He swung the stick again and it shattered and broke in half.

Naomi was mopping her eyes with a tiny handkerchief.

"He's better than Dallas." She sobbed. "He's a good man . . ."

Jamie flung the broken stick away.

"Dallas is better than any of them," he shouted, "better'n Jones, better'n Mr. Benedict . . ."

But Naomi had turned and was running toward the wagons where Webster Shaughnessey had straightened up from his work and stood looking at them.

"Better'n any of 'em," Jamie shouted after her. "Any of 'em."

23

BENEDICT'S WAGON STRAINED and moved forward with Webster Shaughnessey handling the reins, Naomi silent beside him. Theodosia Grant's wagon next, driven by Gideon Hassler. Then Mittenthaler in his own wagon with Hassler's two oxen leading, his own remaining animal and Benedict's big black-and-white milk cow behind.

Lydia Hassler halted on the top of the rise and looked back down the long slope. She would never see this place again, the big smooth rock below the tree where little Lucas was buried.

When the others came to their senses they too would load their wagons and move on. Time would pass; a fresh layer of pine needles would cover the grave; winter would come, snow would fall and settle over the lost and silent place.

Tears filled her eyes and ran slowly down her cheeks. She turned and walked on.

*

They were still within the faint sound of the axes when Cantwell pulled up beside Benedict.

"I'm going back," he said, "see if I can't get some of them to change their minds. Lee and Billy, maybe."

"Hell with 'em," Benedict said. "We'll manage."

But Cantwell was right. When the trail got worse they'd be slowed down from sheer lack of manpower; all of them would have to go ahead, clearing saplings and bushes, dislodging boulders, yoking and unyoking his spare team to pull the wagons up the steep grades.

"I'm going back," Cantwell said.

"They made their decision."

"Maybe Jamie'll change his mind. He's sweet on Naomi Grant."

"Dallas'll never let him go, Ben, you know that."

"I'll try."

"Don't go," Benedict said. "You don't understand what you're getting into — they're in a wild mood."

"I've got to try."

"We've all done that, Ben . . . they won't listen. They want to stay there. Tree's only the start of it. There's no law here, remember that, no law except them."

"I'm not worried," Cantwell said.

"You should be."

"Are you?"

"You're damn right. You saw Dallas. He'd have killed me if he'd had half a chance — he wants all of them back there to chop."

"I think you could take him," Cantwell said, smiling. "In a fair fight. We'd have liked to seen you take him back there."

Benedict studied his saddle horn. Cantwell didn't understand. He didn't understand the chopping.

"Don't go back, Ben."

"I'm going," Cantwell said. "I'll be back before you know it."

"You won't be back," Benedict said, "and nobody's going to come looking for you. I'm not leaving these people again. Ever."

Cantwell touched his hat and swung his horse around.

"I'm doing the best thing," he said, and he went down the rutted trail toward the sound of the axes.

Dallas Mecom was the last to drop his axe and walk to the others who had gathered around Ben Cantwell.

Joseph reached up and held the bridle to steady the horse but Cantwell didn't dismount. It was better that they looked up at him.

"I came back to help," he said, nodding his head toward the tree.

"Never did see you work," Billy Black said. The others relaxed and smiled. It was the truth. And Cantwell was a loner. He never asked for help and never gave any. Now he'd changed.

"What in hell you want?" Dallas said.

"You're going about it the wrong way," Cantwell said.

"Go back to Benedict," Dallas shouted. "We don't need nothin' from you."

"Let the man talk," Cheatham said.

Cantwell swung off his horse, pushed through the others and stood between them, holding his arms up, palms out as if they were about to fight, as if he were keeping them apart. They all knew that Dallas and Cheatham didn't get along.

"There's been enough fighting," he said. "Let's get ourselves organized and finish this thing."

"You're right," Van Sciber said. In a dream he'd seen himself chopping forever, the tree growing faster than he could cut, obliterating the letters of his name . . .

"What's on your mind?" Lee Cheatham said.

Cantwell lowered his hands and turned to the tree.

"First thing you got to do is forget this original cut," he said. "Look at it. It's in the wrong place — it's too low. But you couldn't expect much. It was really started by the Hassler boy, wasn't it?"

"Yassir," Joseph said.

"Second thing," Cantwell went on, "there's a two-man saw in one of the wagons — Van Sciber's — we've got to use that as well as the axes."

"He's right," said Billy Black. "Why didn't we think of that saw?"

"I'll get it," Van Sciber said.

"One last thing," Cantwell said. "We've got to organize ourselves, work in shifts. Half the time you're milling around, getting in each other's way, trying to get a crack at it. We've got to set up shifts, work around the clock."

He was finished. He looked at them and knew he'd done it — when they'd cut down the tree they'd choose a new captain. They'd pick him and later on, in California, it'd be a valuable thing to have people say that you led one of the early parties across the sierra.

"I tole you once to git back to Benedict," Dallas said.

The other men turned away suddenly, their faces dull. All except Cheatham.

"It's a free country, Dallas," Cheatham said. "Ben can do what he wants — same as you, same as me."

"I'm staying here," Cantwell said, and he walked slowly to his horse, took the reins from Joseph, and led it toward the spring.

He needed time. Dallas would make mistakes, drive them too hard. He'd work on the others, on Cheatham and Black, win them over and one day Dallas would stand alone. Then he'd take them over the mountain, following Benedict's cleared trail to California.

24

BENEDICT OPENED HIS EYES and lay without moving, studying the mound of glowing embers, the remains of their fire. It was still night but he must get up and feed the animals and get moving at the first light. They still hadn't reached the spot where he and Jamie and Cantwell had waited for Webster. They weren't moving fast enough.

He closed his eyes. During the long night Dallas, in a dream, came to kill him, to prevent the other men from moving on, leaving the tree . . .

He sat up, staring into the darkness, then he was up shivering, piling wood on the glowing embers until the flames rose, outlining the others who lay under the mounds of blankets and buffalo robes. Beyond them the oxen and horses stirred; his milk cow, tied between the wagons, stomped the ground. He walked around and gently kicked Mittenthaler, Shaughnessey, and Gideon

Hassler. They got up without speaking and gathered around the fire, pulling on their coats.

"We've got to abandon a wagon," he said.

They stomped the frozen ground and rubbed their hands over the fire.

"I'm glad you said it," Webster said. "I've been thinking the same thing . . . now that Cantwell — by the looks of things — isn't coming back."

"That's part of it," Benedict said. "Only four of us now. And too few oxen."

They were silent, knowing Benedict was right, but thinking of the wagons they'd pulled across half a continent; each hoping that Benedict would spare his.

"It's best," Oskar Mittenthaler said. The slope was getting steeper, rockier. It would be wiser to use all the oxen on two wagons.

"We'll leave a wagon here," Benedict said. "Fill it with things we can live without. We'll drop one wagon, lighten the other two. Put three yokes on them."

"Whose wagon?" Webster asked.

"Mine."

The women rose and began cooking. The men helped Benedict load the few things he would take in the two wagons, then filled his abandoned wagon with what was heavy and expendable: Naomi's box of books, a Dutch oven, the heavy chest of drawers the Mittenthalers as newlyweds had brought from Germany, a moldboard plow, a keg of nails, a grinding wheel, anything that would lighten the load that the weakened oxen would have to pull up the mountain.

"Now," Oskar Mittenthaler said, looking at the three-yoked wagon, "now, by God, we can run over the mountain."

It was dawn. They gathered around the fire and ate a breakfast of bread and coffee.

Benedict looked at his abandoned wagon. He'd built it himself. It had come all the way from Illinois and some of the ironwork from faraway Shenandoah on an old wagon of his father's.

He stood up. "Let's go."

They moved off, following Mittenthaler, who walked ahead of the two wagons, leading them upward.

Manuel Silvera swung his axe and felt it slice deep into the heartwood. He wondered what year he had cut through. Each ring in the wood of a tree showed a year's growth and now, if he could stop and brush away the chips, he could count how many years they had cut into the tree . . .

Por Dios, what a wasteful thing they did. He'd been a fool that night, drinking too much, taking his axe to prove to Dallas and the others that he was as good as they, a man, a *macho* . . . A child's trick. An act that would serve no purpose except the thrill of destruction, like the killing of bulls. Bulls, too, were huge and, like the tree, beautiful in God's way and yet it was the custom, as old as man, to kill them as they were killing the tree.

If he was alone, if it were not for Inez and Nilda, he would track Jones and take the stallion. Time would not matter. Distance would not matter. He would eventually find the dirty Mountain Man and cut his throat and ride off with his stallion. The animal had been with him since it was very young; it was part of him. He was bitter now, filled with shame and hate; the American had stolen part of him, his pride, his manhood . . .

If he had not tried to find Jones he would have been at the tree when Benedict left. He would be with the good ones — Shaughnessey and the Germans and Mrs. Grant, Gideon Hassler and his wife, Naomi, the friend of Nilda . . . Now, it was too late. If he tried to leave, Dallas would mock him and call him names no man could endure and he would fight for his honor. Mecom would kill him and Inez and Nilda would be left to die on this cursed mountain.

Van Sciber's sharp chisel cut into the soft wood. He worked out of sight of the others, close to the fire scar, working with such concentration that he was unaware of his wife's approach.

He stepped back to study his work and was happy. The letters were deeply cut and skillfully made.

THIS TREE FELLED 1846

J. VAN SCIBER	L. CHEATHAM
D. MECOM	B. CANTWELL
J. MECOM	M. SILVERA
W. BLACK	

"It's wrong," Betty Van Sciber said.

He turned and stared at her, brushing back his long white hair. She shouldn't be around the tree; she should be down at the wagon, doing woman's work.

"Wrong?"

"The date," she said. "It'll take another year."

There was an antagonism between them now that he couldn't quite believe, a gulf that widened a bit each day by ridicule, by subtle rejections.

He shook his head. "We'll do it. You'll see . . ."

"You forgot Joseph," she went on. "Ask your friend Dallas if he has a full name."

"Yes," he said. "I'll add his name. It's only right . . ."

She stepped closer. "Take me away from this place."

"When we're finished."

"Dallas — he's crazy, don't you see? He started this and it got out of hand and he won't admit it."

Van Sciber breathed in deeply and looked around.

"Don't talk like that."

"We can leave now," she said. "There's still time. We can reach Benedict."

"We'll go when it's finished."

"You'll never finish. It's too big. Look at it. It's too big for you."

"We'll do it," he said. "You'll see . . . we'll win."

"Win?"

He turned away and went to the tree and began to cut away more of the thick, shaggy bark, squaring it off. Betty didn't understand. Cutting down the tree wasn't enough; there had to be a record so people would know that they did it.

"I should have left with Benedict," Betty said.

He didn't turn or answer. She stood watching him work and then began to walk down to the wagons, think-

ing of Benedict as she'd seen him those last hours before
they'd reached the tree: a lone figure ahead of them, leading the party up the slope. He was the kind of man John
should be; a man other men liked or respected, a man of
quiet resolve and determination.

She was afraid. John had at last found something to
consume the unsatisfied hunger within him, but it was an
ugly and shameful thing unworthy of his intelligence,
his pride, his great Hudson Valley name. He would
squander his time, his energy and in the end it would all
be for nothing. A waste. If they didn't leave soon the cold
would drive them back down the mountain.

Billy Black and Lee Cheatham pushed back and forth
on the long crosscut saw they'd taken from Van Sciber's
wagon. It had been sharpened and greased but it caught
in the wood and their progress was slight.

"Your arm's goin' dead, Billy," Cheatham said. "Quit."

"I'm jus' warming up."

"You looked whipped to me."

"Hell," Billy said. "Saw's doin' all the work."

But at last they did stop, leaving the saw quivering in
the cut, walking away from the tree, flexing their arms
and arching their backs, heading toward the spring.

"You're a damn fool," Lee said. "You know that, don't
you?"

"Mebbe so," Billy said. "But I want to see her fall. Van
Sciber said it's the biggest tree in America. Said we'll all
be famous."

"I should've gone on," Cheatham said. "That's the
sensible thing to do. I oughta be with Benedict."

"You promised my Pap."

Cheatham shrugged. "Maybe that's it — but when we left we were goin' to war . . . it's different now."

"Maybe there'll be fightin' in California. Sure hope so. Old Polk can't just take it away from them Mexicans without them fightin'. I'm hopin' there'll be war there too."

"Damn the war," Cheatham said. "Ain't you glad I talked you out of goin'?"

"No," Billy said. "I'm thinkin' of all those people back home. My people. Your people. All the rest. Us braggin' about joinin' up and takin' a crack at them Mexes and all. Goddamn it, Lee. What'll they think when they hear we ain't in Mexico, that we ain't even in the army?"

"There's a lot that don't favor this war," Lee said. "Plenty of good men sayin' it's a bad war, that we ain't got no right killin' them people and gettin' ourself hurt in the bargain."

"You sound like Webster," Billy said. "He was hounded out of some town for talkin' against it."

"I think he's right," Lee said. "The damn war'll lead to more bad blood between North and South."

"Webster's a Yankee."

"He's a smart fellow," Lee said. "He's worried about what it might do, worried that the States will split apart over it and maybe fight each other."

"Damn," Billy said. The thought of it filled his mind.

They walked the rest of the way to the spring in silence, then drank the cool, clear water from their cupped hands.

Tiny ground squirrels chattered and darted around

them. They lay back and looked at the sky, then closed their eyes; the sun was warm on their faces but tonight, they knew, it would be cold. Summer was gone.

The sound of the chopping came to them. It never stopped. Dallas hadn't organized them as Cantwell wanted, but there was, it seemed, always someone cutting into the tree, night or day.

"Why are we doing it, Billy?" Lee asked without opening his eyes.

"Damn," Billy said. "I don't know . . . ask Dallas. I mean we just started and now it's too late to just quit."

"It's stupid," Lee said. "All those years, just standin' there, hurtin' nothin' or nobody, just knowing the sun and the rainstorms and the sky, looking down at the desert and up the other way to those high peaks . . . I swear, Billy, cuttin' her down just ain't a thing a man oughta want to do."

"It's a tree," Billy said. "It's big but it's only a tree, just like any of the rest of them."

Except it's different, Lee thought. It was better than all of them.

The next day, just before noon, John Van Sciber dropped his axe and without a word or look at the others got down out of the big cut and began walking awkwardly down the path to the wagons. Then he collapsed and fell face down, and when Manuel Silvera reached him, he was dead.

Betty Van Sciber knelt down beside him. Tears filled her eyes and ran down her cheeks but she made no sound.

The others gathered behind her. Inez Silvera, praying aloud in Spanish, Nilda standing beside her father, Billy Black and Lee Cheatham and Joseph, Jamie Mecom flushed now with a slight fever. Ben Cantwell, his clothes dirty, looking older.

She stood up, brushing away her tears with a tiny handkerchief. She took a deep breath, steadied herself, and faced the others.

"He's gone," she said. "There's nothing any of us can do. It was his heart. He wasn't young . . . he shouldn't have worked that hard."

None of the others spoke. Nilda Silvera was sobbing and her mother went to her and spoke quietly in Spanish.

"I wanted to go on," Betty said. "We had words over it. He wanted the tree to fall — wanted people to know he had something to do with it . . ."

She turned and looked down at the body. Death had already changed his fine features. He was different now, smaller, older, a stranger. She had been his wife but she had never known him, understood him.

The next morning the body was carried down the slope to the big rock, a graveyard now, where Lucas Hassler and John Blue were buried.

Ben Cantwell performed the brief service, reading from Van Sciber's own Bible, then leading the others in prayer.

Joseph and Manuel Silvera reached for their shovels and Betty Van Sciber turned and walked away, following Dallas Mecom to his wagon.

"Leave now," she said. "Take us over the mountain."

Dallas nodded. "I'll take you, Mrs. Van Sciber."

"Now."

"When I'm finished here."

"You can have the oxen," she said. "All his equipment
. . . leave now. I beg you."

"I'm goin' need them animals."

"Now?"

"When the tree goes down . . . then we'll go on, over
the damn mountain."

She turned away and walked to her wagon, her dark
eyes vacant. She might have been able to convince John
to go on with Benedict; he'd be alive now, high on the
mountain, closer each hour to California.

"Madness," she said quietly. "Madness . . ."

25

WEBSTER SHAUGHNESSEY AND GIDEON HASSLER halted their wagons and walked up the slippery rock-strewn slope to stand with Benedict and Mittenthaler studying the break in the granite cliff that blocked their way.

"It's not any too wide," Hassler said. He was exhausted. The sweating and the cold wind had started the pain in his left shoulder. He began to rub it, then dug his fingers into the long thin muscles of his upper arm. They said it was always warm in California. The older a man got the more he took to the sun to ease his complaints.

"It'll look wider when we clear out the growth," Benedict said. "Cantwell and I went up and it's not as narrow as it looks from down here. We'll cut those trees down, clear away the loose rock and fill in the holes and low spots to keep the wagons from tipping. It'll be tight goin' but we can do it."

"A good day's work by the look of it," Mittenthaler said. "Trees are small but old and tough, branches low to the ground, hard to chop. How many axes we got? Dallas stole mine. I have only a hatchet."

"I've got two," Benedict said. "Two of us can use 'em, others on the rocks and holes. We'll eat and get to it."

"How long?" Webster asked.

"All today, half of tomorrow before both wagons are up," Benedict said.

"I'll take one of those axes and get started," Webster said. Benedict hadn't taken his eyes off the cliff, hadn't looked at any of them. His speech was easy but he was worried about the time lost. If Cantwell hadn't turned back or some of the others had come, Benedict would have sent them on ahead to clear the way and save a precious day.

Jamie Mecom sat with his back against the stump of an evergreen that years before had been struck by lightning and was now gray and splintered, rotting at its base. He held his rifle across his outstretched legs and studied the sky above, thinking about the big bird, waiting to kill it.

The sound of the axes, muffled by the distance and the dense forest, echoed up the mountainside, reverberating until it sounded as if a dozen men were chopping. The late morning sun was warm on his face but the ground was still hard and cold from the night.

He closed his eyes; he was tired and should be sleeping but more than sleep he wanted to kill the eagle, to watch it falter high above as his bullet struck it and then plummet downward . . .

He opened his eyes. Yesterday the eagle had returned to the tree, hovering over it, watching them, it seemed, graceful and unafraid, circling slowly on great broad wings that barely moved. If it came again, his spot by the dead stump would be the most likely place. The sky was more open than any place around the campsite, the top of the big tree closer. Chances were the eagle wouldn't return until they left but if it did he might be lucky and get one good crack at it. Jones, with all he'd done, had never killed an eagle, he'd said so once or twice.

He closed his eyes again and saw Naomi's face, streaked with tears, heard his own voice telling her that he'd never leave Dallas now . . .

When he opened his eyes again he knew that he'd fallen off and slept for some time. The sun had moved higher in the cloudy sky leaving him in the shadow. The rifle had slid off his legs. Chipmunks frolicked around a slab of rock six feet away. He was cold.

He stood up slowly, rubbing the soreness in the small of his back. He went down the slope, to the tree, put his rifle aside, and took Ben Cantwell's axe.

"What in hell you doin' up there?" Cantwell asked.

"Waitin' for that eagle."

"What eagle?"

"One that's got a nest up in this tree — I was the first one that spied him."

"No sense in that."

"Like to pot him real good," Jamie said. "See him come floppin' down."

"Thought you liked birds," Cantwell said, mopping his sweaty face.

"I guess I did — but I'd like to shoot that eagle."

"You don't look well, Jamie. You look feverish."

"I'm good enough."

"You get yourself in bed, boy . . . let this choppin' go."

Jamie swung the axe and watched it bite into the great raw wound. When the tree finally fell, the eagle's nest would go with it. The damn bird might as well be dead.

Theodosia Grant handed a cup of hot soup to Naomi and she tasted it, then pulled a heavy patchwork quilt around her shoulders and moved closer to the fire. The girl was chilled, shivering, unable to stop.

"You'll feel better after this," Theodosia said. "You're plain famished."

"I'm cold," Naomi said. "Chilled to the bone."

"We'll be pushing on any time," Benedict said. "Soon as Oskar checks his wagon."

They were about ready to move. The wagons had been repacked and more things had been discarded. The oxen had been fed a small portion of grain and shelled corn and they were stomping the ground now, blowing steam in the cold air. It was windless, the sky the color of lead.

They sat around a small fire that Lydia Hassler had built. The men had worked the two wagons up the dangerously narrow break in the cliff. The oxen had been driven up, one at a time, and yoked together. Then, with one long chain, each wagon had been slowly pulled up by the combined power of the animals, steadied on each side and guided with great caution by Webster and Gideon Hassler.

Naomi swallowed another spoonful of the hot soup. She wished she'd never come on such a silly trip. It was too long and the guide books were filled with lies. The men spent all their time fighting. And now they were lost in this God-forsaken country where no civilized man had ever been.

"I've finished with the plants," Theodosia said. "Wrapped them with whatever there was — clothing mostly — and packed them in the trunks."

"Will they really live?" Naomi asked. She wished she could be wrapped in blankets, hidden in a huge warm trunk until it was all over, until they were over the mountain where it was never cold, where flowers bloomed at Christmas.

Theodosia held her hands over the fire and looked at Webster. "I don't know. It was the only thing I could think of. They can't die — not all of them."

"They'll live," Webster said. "Some have to live."

The talk of flowers made Naomi think of Nilda Silvera. They had become friends one special day, walking together with the heat of the summer sun on their backs, stopping to pick flowers that grew beside the rutted trail. Nilda, that day, had woven the long-stemmed daisies into a circle and hung the garland around the neck of her favorite mule. The sight of it made them laugh until tears came, until they could no longer walk, until they held each other and slumped into the tall grass . . .

Without warning, big fluffy snowflakes began to fall. They looked up at the darkening sky, at Patrick and Jesse Grant who turned from the fire and ran off, laughing, trying to catch each elusive flake.

Webster thought of home: snow outside of the window of his bedroom as he sat reading, the lamplight penetrating the blackness of the night. His eyes would stray from the fine print of the book to the flakes, swirling in the wind like crazy moths . . . Now the snow frightened him.

"Snow," Gideon Hassler said simply. "Just like you said . . ."

"Sooner than I thought," Benedict said. "I wish we had a few days more."

Oskar Mittenthaler came up to the fire. "I'm ready," he said.

"This snow," Webster said. "We could move faster with one wagon . . ."

Benedict nodded. "Let's wait. See what it's going to do. It might just be a flurry . . . let's wait before we make any more decisions."

Webster was right but the two wagons carried all they had in the world, the tools and seeds and clothing they'd need in California. The wagons would keep Naomi and the two Grant boys out of the snow, keep them warm.

He swallowed the last of the hot bitter coffee Lydia Hassler had brewed and walked toward the Grant wagon. The others followed, leaving the fire as it was, fighting a losing battle with the falling snow.

26

THE WIND CAUGHT THE SNOW, swirling it around the great tree, around the wagons, around the fire. In the corral the oxen moved closer together, turning their heads from its force.

Lee Cheatham stopped chopping. He held out his hand, caught one heavy snowflake and watched it as it melted. Then he swung the axe once more into the wood, left it there as he crawled down out of the cut, leaving Joseph still swinging his axe.

He walked to the fire and looked across it to Billy Black who sat on a flat stone, his trooper's hat pushed back on his head, staring into the flames and blowing on his bare hands. Betty Van Sciber, Ben Cantwell, Jamie Mecom, and Silvera looked at him without speaking.

"I'm going, Billy," he said.

Billy looked up. The snow would most likely fall all day and all night. It worried him.

"If you're comin', come," Lee said. "If you're stayin', good-bye."

Billy nodded. He'd been with Lee as long as he could remember, since they were small boys. When they set off together to fight the Mexicans they'd promised their parents they'd stick together, no matter what.

"I'm stayin'," Billy said. He dropped his head and stared into the fire.

"What the hell you mean, stayin'?"

"I ain't runnin' off again."

"Again?"

"The war," Billy said. "You smart talked me out of joining up jus' 'cause you didn't have the stomach for fightin' — now you want me to run off again."

Lee shook his head. "The war's one thing, Billy," he said. "This damn tree's something else."

"Well, I ain't goin'."

Jamie stood up and walked away, down the slope to the wagons.

"He's going for Dallas," Betty Van Sciber said.

Lee nodded. Jamie was getting more like his brother every day.

"You'd best come with me," he said to her.

"Dallas'll never let you leave," she said. "You should have gone last night."

He turned to Manuel Silvera. "You?"

The other man shook his head. It was a fight now with Dallas Mecom, *mano a mano*.

"I stay."

Lee turned back to Billy.

"We've always been together."

Billy looked up. "You can't quit now. Look at that tree. All that work. All that sweat. You just can't go running off now . . ."

"It's still early," Lee said. "This snow probably won't last — but it's a warning. You better forget this damn tree and start moving or you'll never see California. You'll be forced down into the desert and starve or you'll get trapped here, get yourself frozen stiff as a poker."

"I'm stickin'," Billy said. "I ain't goin' runnin' off from something we all started."

"You didn't start it," Lee said. "Dallas did."

"He's coming now," Betty Van Sciber said.

Dallas came up the slope with Jamie behind him. He wore a heavy red shirt and was still buttoning it when he reached the fire.

"You goin' somewhere, Cheatham?"

"California."

"We're all going there — in good time."

"I'm goin' now," Lee said. The wind had suddenly died and the big snowflakes fell gently.

Dallas smiled and brushed back his long yellow hair.

"We got to hold on here, boy," he said. "Hold on 'til she comes down . . . you suppose to be choppin', ain't you?"

"It's over, Dallas. You said it wouldn't snow for another month. Benedict was right. You want to stay, stay. I'm following Benedict's trail."

Dallas stopped smiling. He turned and looked at Ben Cantwell, then at Manuel Silvera and Jamie.

"This boy's fixin' to desert me."

"I stayed here to be with Billy," Lee said. "Not for you, not for your damn tree."

Dallas nodded to himself.

"Runnin' out. Desertin' us . . . a little bit of snow and you want to go runnin' off lookin' for Benedict."

"He can do what he wants to," Betty Van Sciber said. "We should all go — after it stops snowing."

Dallas stared at him.

"I'm going now," Lee said. "While I can still follow the trail."

"We're goin' to hold on here," Dallas said. "Every mother's son of us. We started something and we're goin' to finish it out."

"Not me," Lee said. "I'm leavin'."

Dallas shrugged. "One thing, Cheatham. Before you go runnin' off on us — I'm goin' to stick a knife in you."

There was a thick-bladed knife in his hand, held straight out.

"*Stop* it!" Betty Van Sciber screamed.

Lee backed away, his eyes never leaving Dallas, moving toward an axe handle that someone had left lying on the ground. He bent down and picked it up.

"Nobody leaves this goddamn tree," Dallas shouted.

"Put the knife away," Cantwell said. "We can settle this like gentlemen."

Joseph stopped chopping.

"Leave him be," Billy Black said.

But Dallas moved around the fire toward Lee who backed off, crouching, holding the axe handle before him.

"He's crazy," he said to the others. "Can't you see that

. . . he'll stay here . . . you'll never get over the mountain."

Ben Cantwell hurried toward them. This was the moment, his moment. Dallas had lost control. He held out his arms and moved between the two men, facing Dallas.

"Put that knife away."

Neither man seemed to see him. He had momentarily blocked their view of each other and they stepped sideways, careful of their footing on the film of snow. But Cantwell followed with outstretched arms, moving closer to Dallas.

"Stay away from me," Dallas said quietly.

Cantwell glanced at the others. Mrs. Van Sciber. Young Billy Black. Jamie Mecom. Manuel and his wife and daughter. Not many, but enough to form his own party.

"I'll take that knife, Mecom."

Dallas lunged forward, driving the knife into the center of Cantwell's chest. In the same instant he slipped and was thrown off balance.

Cheatham sprang forward and whipped the axe handle down on Dallas Mecom's head and he fell heavily, face down.

Betty Van Sciber was screaming. Ben Cantwell sat staring up at them, a look of surprise on his pale face. He clutched his chest where blood welled through his fingers. Then he fell backward and lay without moving, snowflakes settling on his face, his neat mustache.

Jamie Mecom knelt down beside him, then turned, wordless, looking up at the others.

Lee tossed the axe handle aside. Cantwell was dead and there wasn't one goddamn thing any of them could do about it.

"You better come with me," he said to Betty Van Sciber.

She stared at him without speaking. He walked to her and took her arm.

"Get your things, Mrs. Van Sciber. I'll saddle your horse."

"No," she said. "I don't want to go . . ."

"You must come, Mrs. Van Sciber."

"I won't leave. Go. Alone."

Ten minutes later he rode off up the trail that the snow had almost covered, his hat pulled low, the collar of his beaverskin coat turned up to ward off the swirling snow.

27

NAOMI LAY IN THE WAGON as it jolted along in the semi-darkness of the late afternoon, through the light snow that fell from the windless sky.

The wagon stopped. The wind tore at the canvas overhead. Patrick and Jesse, bulky in their coats and buried under mounds of blankets, were asleep in their narrow beds at the front of the wagon.

Webster Shaughnessey brushed aside the flap and looked down on her. She sat up, shocked by the cold air.

"Are we stopping?"

"Not yet," he said. "Not while the snow's still coming down. Not while it's still light."

"Is something wrong?"

"No. They're just looking at something up ahead."

"Are they going to abandon the Mittenthalers' wagon?"

"Benedict says we'll wait and see."

If the snow didn't stop they'd have to abandon both wagons. She wouldn't last long . . . she wasn't strong enough to walk all day through the snow like Aunt Theodosia and Anna Mittenthaler and Lydia Hassler.

Webster ducked through the canvas flap and crouched near her, blowing on his hands. He had a beard now, flecked with snow, and he looked much older than the first time she'd seen him, sitting under a shade tree at the gathering spot outside of Independence, reading a small leatherbound book, shooing flies away with his free hand. It seemed a long, long time ago.

"I've been dreaming about the desert," she said.

"It was a bad time."

"But it was warm and now I'm so cold — and I keep thinking of the others back at the tree."

He nodded. She'd been thinking of Jamie. "They're on my mind too."

"They frightened me," she said. "That night — I went up there. I knew it was wrong but I had to see. It was terrible. It was as if they were . . . murdering the tree."

Webster nodded. "We came down the mountain, guided by that big fire, coming up to them before they saw us. It was like a painting of Hell I'd seen in an old book. There was a peculiar feeling in the air. I felt that some of them would have killed us right then and there because we'd surprised them, disturbed them at something they were ashamed of."

"They went crazy," Naomi said.

"No, not crazy. Not by a long shot. There's an impulse, I think, to smash, to annihilate. A hidden thing that comes to the surface now and then. Maybe it's to balance the impulse to create."

"Like the war," Naomi said. All those boys in Missouri, running off to fight in Mexico . . . she'd never understand men. Never. There was a need within them to hurt, to destroy.

Someone was shouting and without a word Webster left her and went back to the driver's seat, closing the flap behind him. He shouted at the oxen and the wagon jolted and began to creak and groan and lurch forward.

She closed her eyes, thinking about Webster. A painting of Hell, he'd said. But he didn't believe there was a Hell and almost convinced her in spite of all she'd been taught. If Satan did exist, Webster had told her more than once, he didn't reign in Hell among the everlasting fires and the cries of the damned; he was close, ever present, maybe part of them as God was. And God was everything and everywhere at once: in the handful of prairie soil, in the desert flower, in the buds and seeds they'd seen forming and growing ripe as they'd moved west; in the sweep of the rain-filled sky, in the magic of birth, of life.

An hour later they halted on the top of a bare ridge overlooking a small frozen lake. Benedict told them that they would have to abandon Mittenthaler's wagon. No one objected. The six strongest oxen were selected and put on Theodosia Grant's wagon. The others, plus Benedict's cow, would join the saddle horses to break down the growing drifts before the lone wagon.

Benedict had told Webster first as they picked their way through the snow.

"Leave both wagons," Webster said. "We'll go on by foot. Faster . . ."

Benedict shook his head. "No."

"We can put Jesse and Patrick on horseback," Webster said. "And Naomi."

"Wagon's all we've got," Benedict said. "The one thing that holds us together. We've all got something in it. Once we drop it we'll break up. Hassler's ready to quit now, lie down and die. We've got to keep one wagon."

"I see what you did," Webster said. "You knew all along we'd never make it with three wagons, didn't you?"

Benedict nodded. "We'll keep the one wagon until the last possible moment."

"Yes," Webster said. "I see it now."

28

J AMIE M ECOM AND M ANUEL S ILVERA swung their axes,
cutting deeper into the tree. The cut was now so high and
wide that they stood within it. They did not talk, even
when they stopped to rest; they did not talk but stood,
staring down at the snow-covered camp, waiting for the
others to come and take the axes so that they could sleep.

It had snowed steadily for a full day and under it the
body of Ben Cantwell lay, still unburied. Silvera had
wanted to bury him next to the big rock, but Dallas would
not allow him to take time away from the tree. Now the
ground was frozen.

The men chopped and the women — Betty Van Sciber,
Inez and Nilda Silvera — cooked and gathered firewood.
During the snowstorm, unable to wander far from the
campsite to gather wood, they had been forced to chop up
the Hassler wagon; now, unless the snow melted, they
would be forced to burn Van Sciber's.

There was enough to eat. Dallas had shot and butch-ered one of Van Sciber's starving oxen. The snow would soon melt, he'd told them; it had been an early freakish, out-of-season fall; by the time they were finished with the tree, the snow would be gone and they would follow Benedict's trail over the sierra.

Now Joseph, the black man, edged away from the wagons and walked slowly up one of the paths that the women, searching for wood, had trampled in the snow. When he was out of sight of the wagons he began to run. They were killing the tree and it was spoilin' them and if he stayed they'd find a reason to beat him, maybe kill him, like last year when Dallas had gone mean with drink and beat him with his fists. Choppin' made Dallas feel good. When he got tired of the tree, he'd come for ole Joseph.

He stopped.

"Where you goin'?" Jamie Mecom said. He was ten feet away, off the trail, sitting on top of a big rock. There was a shiver in his voice as if he'd been sitting in the wind for a long time. He looked thin and white-faced.

Joseph stared at him. He'd thought Jamie was back around the wagons, sleepin', maybe restin'.

"You've got the fever," he said. "You best get to bed."

"Runnin' off," Jamie said. "Runnin' off when Dallas told you not. We thought Billy would try it first."

He slid down off the rock and leveled his rifle.

Joseph nodded. "They're gettin' mean, Mista Jamie. I've got to get away . . . Dallas, he's gonna hurt me . . ."

Jamie shook his head in disgust. "He *told* you not to leave. Didn't he tell everyone that, more'n once?"

"I got to go, Mista Jamie . . . Let me go."

Jamie shook his head. "Dallas needs you."

"Please, Mista Jamie . . ."

"You're goin' back to the tree," Jamie said. "Dallas told me to keep an eye on the rest of them so he could get some sleep. Now here you go runnin' out on him."

"You got the chill, Mista Jamie. You get yourself out of this cold now, out of those wet boots."

"Jones ran off," Jamie said. "Then Cheatham. Dallas says we got to stop this desertin' . . . now you turn around and start back down."

Manuel Silvera, turning from the tree saw them, Joseph first, his body slack, head bowed, then Jamie hunched over, shivering from the cold, carrying his rifle.

Billy Black dropped his axe and whistled. "Sure glad I ain't that nigger. Dallas'll beat hell out of him."

Jamie stopped ten feet from the fire and Joseph slumped down. The rest of them gathered around.

"What's he done?" Betty Van Sciber asked.

"Runnin' off."

"You brought him *back?*"

Jamie stared at her. "He's desertin'."

Dallas Mecom came from his wagon and hurried up the slope, brushing back his long hair. He shouldered past the others and stood, hands on hips, looking down at his slave.

"Runnin' off to join Benedict," he said.

Joseph looked up, his face expressionless. Then he dropped his eyes.

"Tole you nobody leaves here 'til we've finished," Dallas said.

He turned to Jamie. "Why in hell di'n't you shoot him?"

"You can't shoot him for running off," Betty Van Sciber said.

"She's right," Billy said.

Dallas turned to him. "You're right, Billy. I ain't goin' to shoot him. He's a deserter. I'm goin' to hang him."

Billy looked at Joseph and Manuel Silvera and Jamie. "*Hang* him?"

"Goddamn right. That's what they do to deserters, ain't it?"

"You can't hang him," Billy said. "Hanging's for the law. Hanging's for murder and hoss stealin'."

Hanging a man, even a slave, would be a terrible thing, something that would never leave you, something that you'd think about years later, spoiling your dreams, making you afraid when you were half-asleep. And Joseph was one of them now, he'd come the full way.

"He deserted!" Dallas shouted. "You goin' to stand there and say he didn't desert me?"

"Hanging's not for the likes of us," Billy said. "We're ordinary men."

"A bad thing," Silvera said. "We cut the tree. Now we talk of killing each other."

Dallas turned to him. "What you doin' here?"

Manuel Silvera shrugged and began walking back up

the slope toward the tree. There was bad trouble coming. Dallas had murdered Cantwell. Now he was going to hang his slave. Nothing would stop him.

"Wouldn't pay to have trouble about this," Dallas said, turning back to Billy.

"Goddamn, Dallas," Billy said easily. "I'm just saying there's no reason to hang him. Horsewhip, that'd be proper. No hangin'."

"He ran off," Dallas said quietly. "I told all of you nobody leaves until we get this thing done. We'd have hung Jones if we'd been able to catch the bastard and all he did was steal Silvera's horse. This damn nigger deserted me and I aim to hang him."

Jamie nodded to himself. Jones . . . pretendin' to be one thing, and you turned your back and damned if he wasn't something else. He hated Jones now as he'd never hated another man . . . in one of his dreams they'd followed his trail down the mountain and found him. Silvera's stallion had thrown him. He was sitting with his back against a tree, one leg broken, as they closed in on him, torches burning, guns ready. They'd dragged him back to the wagons and built up the fire. Jones was talking, begging for his life, lying faster than a dog could trot, but nobody listened. Cantwell propped up a wagon tongue and he himself pulled the noose over Jones's greasy head, fitted it around his skinny, corded neck . . . *You ain't no Mountain Man, you goddamn horse-thievin' murderer. You ain't no real Mountain Man . . .*

"Get a rope, Jamie," Dallas said. "Get me a rope."

"It's murder," Billy shouted.

Dallas swung around. "I didn't favor that the first time, Billy. You best get back on the tree. You can't get in any trouble up there."

Billy stared at him.

"Wait," he said. "You want that tree to fall, don't you, Dallas? Well, you hang this nigger and you'll have one less man . . ."

Dallas stared at him for a long time, then glanced down at Joseph.

"We'll watch him," Billy said. "Sure as hell, Dallas, we'll put him on the tree, work him 'til he drops, never let him out of our sight. You hang him, we'll never cut 'er down."

Dallas was looking at the tree, watching Manuel Silvera as he picked up his axe, climbed up in the cut and began to chop — a lone man against the giant tree.

Then he looked at Billy Black and began to nod his head.

"You're right, Billy . . . for once you made some sense. Now you take him and put him on that goddamn tree and you keep him there, hear?"

Billy took a deep breath. "I'll work him, Dallas, just you watch . . ."

"You keep him there 'til I tell you different," Dallas said. He turned and kicked at the black man, missing his face by a scant few inches as Joseph ducked.

"I'll work him 'til he drops," Billy said.

Dallas pointed a finger at him. "He runs off again I'll hang you, Billy. Sure as hell I will."

He turned and walked back to his wagon.

Joseph stood up and began to tremble. Tears welled from his eyes. He looked at Billy Black and nodded. Then he hurried up the slope toward the tree.

29

LEE CHEATHAM PUSHED HIS HORSE up the mountain until
the animal was wide-eyed and trembling with exhaustion.
He dismounted and walked, leading the horse through the
snow that fell quietly, relentlessly, a wet snow that hung
on the pine boughs until they slowly bent and dumped it
downward.

He'd lost Benedict's trail. The snow frightened him. It
obscured his vision and made him feel more alone, more
vulnerable, a tiny slow-moving figure lost in the gloom of
the featureless forest. But the snow covered his own
tracks; if Dallas was following him, he would soon give up
and return to the camp.

As the day ended the snow seemed to fall with greater
force, the flakes smaller now, colder, blown by sudden
gusts of wind. It grew dark and he stood close to the animal, shielding himself from the wind. Then he moved

on in darkness that was so complete that he held his left hand before him to ward off the dead branches of the smaller trees. The horse balked. He spoke to it and pulled it on and at last, when he had almost given up, he found himself going downhill, slipping and falling once, stopping at the bottom of a bowllike depression out of the force of the snow-laden wind.

He did not rest. He began to lead the horse around in a small circle, trampling down the snow. A half an hour later he removed the saddle, confident that the animal would stay with him, where it was, sheltered from the direct blast of the wind.

He wrapped himself in his two blankets and curled up below the lip of trampled snow. He fell asleep and when he awoke it was almost dawn and the snow had stopped falling.

He came to the granite ridge that Benedict had told them about. He was off the trail, lost and did not know which way to turn to find the way up. If he could not find it quickly he would have to abandon the search and go on by foot.

He was lucky. On an impulse he turned north and found it, led his horse up the cleared path and rode on.

That night he stopped next to the dry trunk of a great pine that had fallen long ago and now lay in the snow like the skeleton of some huge animal.

The next day he crossed Benedict's fresh trail and drove his horse on, catching up with the party as it fought through a narrow pass where jagged cliffs and gnarled snow-heavy trees leaned outward as if to engulf them.

*

Theodosia Grant handed him a mug of hot soup. He blew on it and sipped it. The others stood around him, close to the small fire, as the frozen snow melted from his beaverskin coat.

"It was a terrible thing," he said, staring into the flames. "As I said, Dallas knifed him as he stood there trying to stop it."

Oskar Mittenthaler nodded. Cantwell murdered by Dallas. It didn't seem shocking now; it was part of the violence unleashed by the chopping. Long ago in Germany he and some other boys had started to torment a lone cow they had found grazing in a high mountain meadow. In the end they had killed it, murdered it, chased the frightened and confused animal until it ran off a cliff . . .

"Saw his eyes," Lee said. "He wasn't mad or anything . . . Dallas killed him, just like that. Knew he'd kill me then, not just cut me up . . ."

"Why didn't Billy come with you?" Webster asked.

Lee shook his head back and forth in a gesture of disgust.

"I'll never know . . . he just made up his mind to stay at the tree. Dallas's got a hold on him . . ."

"Silvera," Benedict said. "I half expected him to follow us . . ."

"He would have left with you," Lee said. "Told me that more'n once. But I guess he knew Dallas would never allow it."

"Jamie Mecom," Theodosia said.

Lee shook his head. "Jamie — he changed. The more time passed, more he got like Dallas."

"Nilda," Naomi asked, "is she all right?"

"Same as ever," Lee said.

"We've got to keep moving," Benedict said. "Storm's over but another one could start any time."

Cheatham drained the cup. "I can help out, now that I'm here."

"No," Benedict said. "You sleep first, in the wagon. Sleep good. Rest of the day. Tomorrow you'll be breaking trail."

They were soon pushing on, Mittenthaler first, feeling a path, then Benedict and Webster Shaughnessey, driving the extra horses and the milk cow to trample down the snow for the lone wagon which Hassler drove.

They came, the next day, to the edge of a granite dome, not sheer, but dangerously steep. A man, moving carefully, could make his way down it but no wagon or animal. It was free of snow except where it had gathered in pockets and around the few twisted trees that clung in crevices. To the north it broke into cliffs; southward the rock ended in a slope, steep and almost bare of trees but deep with drifted snow.

"We'll go down," Benedict said. "Wagon would never get through those drifts and we haven't got the strength or time to dig our way through."

"I agree," Mittenthaler said.

Cheatham, Shaughnessey and Gideon Hassler said nothing. There was another rise ahead but it was not quite as high as the land they stood on. This might be the first

of a series of descents that would get them out of the high
country.

Benedict turned to Webster. "Work your way down
there and look around. There's a lone cedar three quarters
of the way down. See if the tree's strong enough to hold
the weight of the wagon. Be careful. Don't get yourself
killed."

An hour later they began to lower the wagon down the
incline. It had been pulled as close to the edge as
possible, turned around. The long towing chain was fastened on the front axle, then to the solid yoke of the ox
team which was led off by Mittenthaler until the chain
was straight.

Benedict inspected the wagon once more to make sure
that nothing would shift and throw it off balance. Then
he stepped away, grasped one of the wheels and pushed
with Hassler, Webster, Cheatham, trying to get it moving. The women, watching, saw that it was too much for
them and they hurried and added their weight against the
wheels and the wagon slowly moved, over the edge, the
iron rims of the big wheels screeching on the naked rock.

The chain snapped taut as the weight was transferred
to the string of oxen. Then, with Hassler helping him,
Oskar Mittenthaler urged the animals backward, a step
at a time.

Webster and Lee followed the wagon downward, cling-
ing to the side, guiding it as best they could to keep the
wheels level, kicking loose slabs of stone out of the way,
halting the movement entirely once to chop down a small

twisted tree. They were constantly aware of the danger. If the axle broke or the chain snapped, the wagon would hurtle down, sweeping them along unless they had time to scuttle free along the rock; even then the whipping chain, or rocks loosened by it, could sweep them to their death below.

They halted the wagon at a spot Webster had seen when he had first climbed down, a place some ten feet below the ancient cedar that was laterally level; it might be too steep for their purpose but they had no choice.

Webster braked the front wheel. Then, working with Lee, they took the two fresh-cut logs out of the wagon, jammed them under the wheels, and lashed them securely. Then four guy ropes, one on each wheel, were secured, one to the thick tree, one around a lip of rock and the other two around stakes that Cheatham had pounded into a two-inch crevice with a heavy flat stone.

It was done. They moved on hands and knees toward the lone tree. They heard Benedict shout, then held their breath as the chain went slack. The wagon groaned and slid forward. One guy rope snapped. But it held, pushing against the logs that held its wheels.

Benedict began to lower the chain to them. It had been uncoupled from the oxen, the freed end fastened with a rope. Benedict let it descend slowly and they worked it around the gnarled tree. Cheatham untied the rope and waved to Benedict, then began kicking at it until it slithered down the rest of the incline to the snow below.

The wagon stood awkward and vulnerable. If the ropes

snapped or the logs under the wheels slipped, it would hurtle down and be destroyed.

Lee and Webster lay back on the steep rock. All they could do now was to wait.

Benedict was the first down the steep snowfield, fighting through it, urging his horse on, bucking through the deep drift that threatened at times to engulf them.

Gideon Hassler waited until Benedict was down, then he drove the rest of the horses before him, shouting and waving his hat so that the animals would move on and add their weight to crush down the soft snow.

Then Oskar Mittenthaler led the oxen, one yoked pair at a time, and headed them down the widened trail.

Finally, with Patrick Grant on his back he led the women down, Theodosia Grant holding Jesse's hand, Naomi, Lydia Hassler, and his wife, Anna, leading Benedict's cow.

Benedict and Mittenthaler found the end of the chain, refastened it to the yoked oxen and whipped the weary animals until the chain snapped out of the snow, taut and straining.

Lee and Webster, moving cautiously on the steep rock, keeping above the chain in case the tree pulled loose, removed the wheel logs and cut the ropes, watching the tree as it gradually took the full weight of the wagon.

It would hold. They shouted to Benedict. The oxen were moved slowly backward. The chain began to slip around the tree, chewing away the bark, then the reddish wood, and the wagon moved downward.

They did not move on but gathered around a huge fire, drying their clothes, eating a meager meal. Hassler and Benedict removed one of the wagon's rear wheels which had sprung loose from its rim. The iron was badly bent. They heated it red hot in the fire, then hammered it back into shape on a flat rock. When they were finished it was dark; the others had been sleeping, unmindful of the noise of their work.

30

BETTY VAN SCIBER, wearing her husband's pants and boots and sealskin coat, took her remaining food and started up the mountain. She walked slowly, keeping under the trees where the snow was hardest, following the faint trail made by Lee Cheatham's horse. In the pocket of the coat was her husband's pistol. She had promised herself that if Dallas followed her, she'd shoot him dead before he spoke the first word. Halfway through the morning Dallas had rummaged through her wagon, found a bottle of her husband's whiskey, and begun to drink; two hours later he'd crawled into his wagon, burrowed under his buffalo robes and fallen into a drunken sleep.

She had left the others without speaking to them and they watched her go up the mountainside until she vanished among the trees.

Billy Black dropped his axe and got down out of the big cut and hurried to get his heavy coat, his rifle, the few things he could carry. If a woman had the courage to leave, he too must leave. They should have all left with Lee, when Dallas had killed Ben Cantwell, when Dallas lay unconscious in the falling snow . . .

Now, he had no horse. The day after Lee had left, Dallas had turned all the horses loose from the corral and chased them off, shouting, waving his arms, then firing his rifle until the last of them had bolted through the snow, down the mountain. Now, none of them could get far if they sneaked off, deserted him.

He started up the mountain, following the path that Betty Van Sciber had broken through the snow.

Joseph sat by the fire watching Billy as he gathered his belongings and started up the mountain. Only three left to chop now.

Dallas wouldn't quit. Never. He'd make them chop until they got sick like Jamie or dropped dead like Mr. Van Sciber. Dallas would stay at the tree until it fell no matter what happened to the rest of them.

He left the fire and went down to the wagon where Dallas lay sleeping. Five minutes later, carrying his axe, wearing Cantwell's boots and a coat made from a buffalo robe, he started up the long white slope.

Manuel Silvera left the tree and walked to his wagon. His wife and daughter lay inside, fully awake, trying to keep warm under their blankets.

Van Sciber's woman and Billy had left without a word. Then the black man. They were afraid of each other now.

There was no concern. No trust. The tree had robbed them of it.

"We'll go now," he said. "The boy and the slave have followed the woman up the mountain."

Inez Silvera's eyes widened. "Where is Dallas?"

"Drunk. Very drunk. He sleeps."

Inez sat up and slapped at the mound of blankets that hid her daughter.

"Hurry," she said. "We must get away . . ."

The girl sat up.

"The mules . . . can we take our mules?"

"No," Manuel said. "We must leave them — there's no time for the mules. We'll take our money. Food. Nothing else."

Nilda's eyes filled with tears, then she began to sob as she got up. Jones had stolen their beautiful stallion and now they would abandon their mules. The mules were like people. When Dallas discovered that they'd run off he would kill the mules, murder them.

"Hurry," her mother said. "Hurry."

Twenty minutes later, on top of the first rise above the camp, they halted in the deep snow to catch their breath and looked back at the forlorn campsite. The fire still burned, the smoke merging into the mist that hung over the mountain.

"Go back," Inez said to Manuel. "Kill him or he'll follow us . . ."

Manuel looked at her, seeing a hardness that had never been there before.

"Kill him, Manuel. He'll track us. He's an animal, a devil. He'll find us, kill us."

Manuel turned away. He could not murder a man in cold blood even if it was Dallas Mecom.

"Do it," she said.

"God forgive us," he said, and turning back to her, he did something that he had not done in many years. He blessed himself.

"Give me the pistol," she said.

"No."

"I have a knife."

He shook his head. No.

She held out her hand. "The gun, Manuel."

He opened the pack, found his pistol. It was loaded. She had fired it many times.

She took it and walked away, back down the slope, moving carefully along the narrow trail.

Manuel sat down beside his daughter on a fallen tree trunk.

"Forgive me," he said to Nilda. "I could not kill a man that way . . ."

Nilda was crying. In some ways women were stronger than men. No woman would have cut into the tree. Her father had done it because he was a man of great pride and a man such as that would never kill another man unless they were evenly matched. Men did not care about life. Women had no pride.

Her mother vanished among the wagons. Nilda did not look at her father. Soon there would be a terrible sound, a deadly crack and she would jump a little and Dallas Mecom would be dead.

"It was a sin," Manuel said. "Cutting the tree. Many

would say that it is not. Many priests. All priests. But it was a sin."

Nilda nodded her head.

"I was lost," Manuel said. "I did not tell the Americans. I was lost but the tree saved me. I lost the track of that stinking Jones. My horse was lame. I had no food. I turned back and came up the mountain and soon I knew that I was lost. I was frightened. I thought of you, of your mother. Then I knew that if I climbed high enough I might see the top of that great tree . . ."

"And you saw it?" Nilda asked.

"Far away. I had drifted south because the land, the forest is the same. Far away I saw the top of our tree and I began to weep with joy — real tears, Nilda, and I was not ashamed. The tree saved me."

"She's coming back," Nilda said.

Manuel turned his head and watched his wife ascend the slope, one slow, deliberate step at a time, until at last she stood before them, breathless, holding the pistol in front of her.

"He was in his wagon," she said to him. "I looked at him. I pointed the pistol at his head . . ."

She caught her breath.

"His life was over . . . I started to pull the trigger. Then I heard a noise. The brother. Jamie. The good one. He was there too. Sick. Feverish. Soaked in sweat. I would murder him if I killed the older brother . . ."

Manuel took the pistol. They began walking up the trail that Betty Van Sciber, Billy Black and Joseph had broken through the hard snow.

31

WHEN THE SHORT DAY ENDED and shadows turned black on the frozen snow, Benedict called a halt and they hurried, almost wordless, to make camp. They hadn't stopped moving since they'd left the bottom of the granite dome at dawn. It was bitter cold.

Oskar Mittenthaler started a fire while Anna and Lydia Hassler hurried off to collect dead branches, snapping them off the smaller evergreens. Theodosia Grant began to cook. There were the few last pounds of bacon. There were cornmeal and two tins of crackers, coffee but no sugar, some cheese; during the day Lee Cheatham had moved ahead of them, his rifle ready, looking for game, but without success.

Benedict and Cheatham freed the two weakest oxen from their yokes and replaced them with the pair that had been rested, herded along all day in front of the lone wagon.

It was a pity, Benedict thought, to see animals suffering so, struggling through the crusted snow, whipped and half-starved, then standing all night in the cold, still yoked to the wagon. But it had to be. If a sudden snow flurry came it would take precious time and effort to gather them, yoke them in place.

Benedict turned to Cheatham. "When we get out of here, I'll tell you what I'm going to do. Take my poor animals, let them graze and grow fat the rest of their lives. Feed 'em whatever they like. Fix their feet. Grain every day, even in summer, and a nice cool spot to sleep when it's hot, a good tight barn when it's cold."

Anna Mittenthaler and Theodosia Grant helped Naomi out of the wagon and led her toward the fire. Oskar Mittenthaler had built it against a high flat rock which reflected the heat like a fireplace and she stood letting the waves of heat flow over her.

Webster Shaughnessey brought a box from the wagon and she sat down, still shivering, fighting an urge to cry. They were fighting despair, holding on, each of them, to some slender thread of hope. She was afraid now, more than she'd tell any of them, afraid of the raw jagged peaks that hemmed them in, brooding and grotesque, rising up to the threatening sky.

Patrick and Jesse Grant had joined the others in collecting fuel, piling their wet sticks separate from those of the adults, running off to find more. Naomi watched them. They thought it was a game.

"I'm cold," she said. "Even with the fire."

"A good meal," Webster said. "That's what you need." During the day he had talked with Benedict about killing one of the animals — the milk cow or Oskar Mitten-thaler's ox or even one of the horses. They couldn't go much farther without food, without one heavy meal each day, without meat. Benedict hadn't agreed; he'd listened and nodded and walked on, a farmer who might starve himself to the point of death rather than slaughter a precious animal.

Naomi reached out and found his hand, held it in a tight grip.

"Stay with me, Webster," she said without looking up at him. "Talk . . ."

He knelt down beside the box, facing the fire. "Maybe tomorrow we'll take a turn and we'll know we're out of this, we'll be moving down, out of the cold, rollin' down to California . . ."

She looked at him, his head in profile as he talked. His sharp features were blurred now beneath a black beard and long hair that half covered his ears. He was drawn and weary but there was determination in his face and she knew that he was stronger, better than Jamie Mecom and all the others who'd let Dallas bully them into staying at the tree.

Benedict called to Lee Cheatham and Oskar Mitten-thaler and they came to stand by him in the failing light, stoop-shouldered, stamping their feet, knocking one frozen boot against the other, clenching and unclenching their gloved hands, dull-eyed from fatigue, their beards filled with tiny globes of ice.

"We've got to eat," Benedict said. "Eat as much as we can . . . I'll have to kill that ox of yours, Oskar."

Mittenthaler nodded. His thin face was bearded now, his cheeks and forehead scoured by the cold wind.

"Yes, kill it."

"It's either the ox or my milk cow."

"Kill it."

"I'm sorry," Benedict said.

They led the ox within the ring of light cast by the fire. Its hip bones were pushed outward against tight-drawn hide. Mittenthaler turned away. Lee Cheatham shot it through the head with his hunting rifle. Benedict came with a heavy knife and began to butcher the carcass as the others dragged logs and chopped wood.

Two hours later they were still around the big fire, warm and dry for the first time since the preceding night, as stuffed with meat as they could remember.

Benedict stood up. "We'll move soon as the first light comes," he said quietly. "This last blow was just a warnin' — like old man winter meant to scare you, telling you a real blizzard was coming."

The heat of the fire had dried Oskar Mittenthaler's wet pants and sodden boots; now the flames scorched his face. He had no wagon, no animals, but his tools were in the wagon and Anna was with him. They had come a long way together, long in time, long in distance. He reached out and found her hand.

She looked up and smiled. *"Kennst du das Land . . ."*

He nodded and squeezed her hand. Yes. The land where the lemon trees bloomed, where the soft wind blew . . . The hot meat and the fire had revived them. Soon the snow and the endless forest would be behind them. They would be safe in the warm valley of California.

Gideon Hassler winced and closed his eyes. He had sprained his back and the cold was in it. Now, he'd give a thousand dollars for a good night's sleep in a real bed.

"I wonder if they did it," Webster said. "Cut it down."

Gideon Hassler found it hard to remember the great tree, as if it was too big for the mind, as if it was part of some child's dream, as if it hadn't been there at all.

"I figger they're still at it," Lee said finally.

He tossed an ice-covered stick into the fire and watched it as the ice melted and the stick caught fire. On the second or third day, when he got bored doing nothing he'd picked up an axe and begun cutting — then suddenly he felt what the other men must have felt all along, a secret, furtive happiness, a deep shameful joy at cutting into the great tree.

32

MANUEL SILVERA KNELT close to the tiny fire praying,
quietly saying each word, trying to forget the coldness
within him, the hunger, the despair. He had grown away
from his religion. He had never been one to spend much
time on his knees but now there was nothing else. Only
the endless snow falling, the great, unbelievable drifts
and the bitter wind. If God did not help them soon they
would all be dead.

It had taken the six of them two exhausting days and
most of two nights to reach the ridge and struggle up the
narrow path which Lee Cheatham had negotiated.

They had hurried on under the brooding trees when,
with no warning, the blizzard struck.

First it was only a sound, a slithering glassy noise of ice
needles whispering over the frozen snow, swirling around
their feet, stinging their faces as they pulled down their

hats and turned their heads. Then, as the wind built up, the icy whispering became a great moaning, a sound that terrified them, caused them to hurry, to trip and fall awkwardly, breaking through the frozen surface of the old snow, thrashing in the loose snow underneath as the ice needles scoured their faces, blinded them.

The sky became dark. Billy Black gathered them together, shouted that they must hold on to each other; he led them on, staggering against the wind that grew stronger each minute until one gust knocked them down, crushing them into the swirling snow.

Billy dragged them on, one heavy step after another, until they reached a big concave rock. They slumped down out of the blasting wind and began to dig down through the snow, throwing it up, burrowing down to hide from the wind. Only then did they discover that Joseph was not with them.

They had not left the cavelike shelter of the big rock. The snow had not stopped; now they could barely fight their way across the deep drifts to break dead branches off the pine trees for their tiny fire.

Betty Van Sciber dropped a few wet twigs on the fire and wondered how Manuel Silvera could kneel so long and mumble the same words over and over again.

Inez Silvera and her daughter slept, hugging each other under their blankets. Billy Black, his head invisible under his soldier's hat, lay next to them. They told each other it was best to sleep and rest, to wait for the snow to end, but their eyes were dull and their voices strange.

She sat back and watched the flames lick at the wet twigs. It was over now, the whole mad suicidal venture. John was dead and the party was destroyed and Dallas was back at the tree, alone now except for Jamie.

She'd stayed at the tree because Dallas stayed. None of the others had known that, certainly not John, but it was true. She could admit it now, think about it without shame. Dallas could have had her, could have taken her anytime and he would have except for his obsession with the tree. That much was clear now: Dallas had been drawn to the tree as she'd been drawn to him. He'd reverted, followed the primal urge to destroy in the same way that she'd turned from her husband and all she'd known to possess the destroyer.

And now the end. Silvera's God would never come. They were trapped, hemmed in by snowdrifts ten feet high, hopelessly lost without food or fuel. The Furies had overtaken them. They had destroyed themselves.

33

THE BLIZZARD, THEODOSIA KNEW, had passed over them and they were at last moving down the long western slope of the sierra, each wheel turn taking them away from the savage peaks, the gloomy passes blocked with snow.

She lay in the wagon, hugging her two sons, listening to the muffled talk of Webster Shaughnessey and Naomi; Webster drove and Naomi walked beside the wagon.

She thought of Benedict. He was ahead of the wagon, limping forward, wearing a wool coat that had been her husband's, a bandana tied over his battered black hat, knotted under his chin. Now he rarely spoke; he looked at them with a great weariness but said nothing unless they asked him something. He'd stood before Dallas Mecom and refused to fight. He was an uncommon man. When they reached California, she would be his wife.

At dawn, standing beside him as he ate, she had studied his bearded face, the tremor in his hand.

"You must hate Dallas," she said suddenly.

He looked at her, frowning slightly.

"No. I don't hate him."

"Were you afraid of him?"

"Yes. If I hadn't left, he would have killed me."

"They stayed there, just like you said they would. Turned against each other. How did you know?"

Benedict nodded and turned and stared at the mist-shrouded peaks behind them.

"It was a long time ago," he said quietly. "Someday I want to tell you all of it . . . slavery men against the others. I was young — almost a boy. One night I joined a bunch of men. The leaders said we'd throw a scare into some of them on the other side. It started out one thing, ended up another. When it was over there were men shot dead, plain farmers like ourselves, murdered by torchlight in their own yards . . . we were all righteous, we were all good. But we killed, maimed each other. My foot — that's why I limp: the other side caught me some time later. Wanted me to talk. Tied me up. One of them took a knife . . ."

He turned back to her.

"A man like Dallas — he's no stranger to me."

"Could he catch up with us?" she asked.

Benedict looked at the forest-covered slopes.

"We've got to figure he will. Got to be ready."

They were moving downhill, the oxen smashing a path through the crusted snow, not so deep now, trampling it down. In the boxes and chests, her plants had survived, wrapped in woolens, protected from the freezing winds.

In California they would find rich soil to germinate and bloom and multiply and fill the land with their seed.

When they stopped for the night they discovered that Gideon Hassler was no longer with them. They looked at each other, at the darkening forest around them.

"He was walking behind the wagon," Lydia said. "Not long ago. He can't be too far behind us . . ."

Benedict took Lee Cheatham by the arm.

"Go back and help him along. We'll get the fire started."

It worried him. Hassler had barely spoken a word all day.

Cheatham turned away, walking back along the wide trail that the oxen and the wagon had crushed through the snow. He was suddenly alone, fighting the small fears that rose in him, wishing that Webster had come with him. It would soon be dark and yet he could not go back without Mr. Hassler and there was no telling what he'd done or what might have been done to him.

It was by accident that he saw Gideon Hassler sitting on the hard surface of the snow, off the trail, back against a tall tree, legs out straight, hands in the pockets of his coat. He was startled and felt that the other man would have let him walk on and not called out to him.

"Came lookin' for you."

"Restin'," Hassler said. "I fell pushing the wagon. Lay for a spell while the rest of you went on . . ."

Cheatham walked over to him.

"You go back," Hassler said. "I'll be along in a little bit."

"We've stopped. Got a nice fire goin'. Cookin'."

Gideon frowned. Cheatham had disturbed him. He wanted to rest here alone, away from the others, wanted to think. Mostly think. Godlike, Mittenthaler said. And maybe it was, put there to make them see something . . . and yet they'd destroyed it, each in his own way for his own reason, killing what they couldn't tolerate, smashing down whatever made them feel puny and mean and worthless.

"Mr. Benedict's waitin' for us," Lee said.

Gideon looked up. Benedict. No better man. Somehow, he'd known about the tree. Dallas wanted to kill him. Couldn't tolerate him either.

"I told them to kill the ox," he said.

"Git up now, Mr. Hassler. It's gettin' dark."

"It was me that gave them the go-ahead . . . told them to chop it."

"They'd have done it anyway," Lee said. "Dallas and Jones. Van Sciber. Billy. Wasn't nobody goin' to stop 'em. I was there, remember."

"Went up to stop them," Gideon said. "Sure wish I had. If I'd tried I might have done it . . . just might have . . ."

Lee knelt down in the crusted snow and looked into the pale blue eyes, sunk deep in his skull. He took Gideon's right hand out of his pocket, feeling the coldness, the stiffness, through the torn glove.

"I'm to blame too," he said. "I should have left with you, made that stupid Billy come with me. But I stayed, knowin' it was wrong, maybe sinful . . . tryin' to prove something, I guess . . . You got to stand up now, Mr. Hassler. We've got to get back."

Gideon closed his eyes. They were lost. The next snow would finish them. God would see that they were punished.

"We were wrong, Mr. Hassler," Lee said. "Both of us. Shouldn't have done what we did. But it's over with . . . You bein' a preacher and all, you know we do things we shouldn't. Bad things. We sin. Can't help it — but we can be sorry. That's what I learned. Now you stand up. Mr. Benedict's waitin' for us with the others. Your wife . . ."

Gideon remembered Lydia. He moved his legs and reached up for Cheatham's powerful arms. And began to cry.

34

DALLAS MECOM, standing inside the deep cut, swung his axe and sent another chip flying. He stopped and rested until the chill got to his sweating body. Then he began again, swinging the axe, cutting into the heart of the great tree, thinking that the wood was hardening with the cold, defying the blade of the axe that he sharpened hourly with a file and a worn whetstone. His face was gaunt, hollow cheeked, half-covered by a yellow beard.

The blade hit a sliver of ice that had formed in an old cut. The axe glanced upward, throwing him off balance. He tried to recover but his foot slipped. He fell heavily, throwing the axe away as he arched backward to hit the frozen snow that had drifted almost level with the bottom of the cut. He slid down the drift almost to the fire and lay, trying to catch his breath, wincing from the sharp pain in his sprained arm, knowing that it was over, that he'd never pick up the axe and chop again.

He got up and went down the narrow path to the wagons, half-buried in the drifts, hopeless and forlorn, their whitetops collapsed under the weight of the snow. All the animals were dead in the corral at the bottom of the depression. He shot them one night when their noise disturbed his sleep, the wild-eyed starving oxen and the skeletal mules.

And Jamie was dead, lying in the dark, cavelike shelter they'd made under the wagon to get out of the wind, dead from the fever and the cold, after one last night of delirium, sweating and mumbling about their mother and their farm, talking wildly about Jones, about Naomi, about the eagle he had tried to shoot.

He found his rifle and his heavy belted coat, then stuffed a bag with frozen meat he'd chopped from one of the carcasses. The mountain rose before him, vast and threatening, glistening silver, the crest lost in the mists that hung below the leaden sky.

He pulled on a pair of stiff gloves and flexed his fingers, then turned and began walking down the mountain, down the way they'd come so long ago, down to the desert where the cold couldn't reach him, where he'd find food, where he'd survive.

35

BENEDICT HAD GOT THEM moving early, almost before dawn, and they were again making their way down the western slope. They were ragged and hungry but they were out of danger. The snow, the bitter cold was behind them. Soon, he thought, maybe before the day ended, they would come to a place where the forested mountain fell away, where they would suddenly see the warm, green California land lying before them.

Now, walking alone ahead of the wagon, he suddenly stopped. A wide band of sunlight slanted down, piercing the gloom, illuminating the beauty and power of the spot. He was overwhelmed. He stood still.

Webster and Lee Cheatham, walking fifty feet behind, stopped at almost the same instant, cutting off their quiet talk. They stood as the sunlight seemed to expand, to fill the glade.

"My God," Webster said, "my *God* . . ."

Then he began to laugh. Looking upward, forgetting the others, he laughed deeply, pulling off his faded hat and swatting it against his thigh.

Lee Cheatham stared at him, smiling, rubbing his bearded chin, nodding his head. Then he began laughing.

Benedict looked up and around at the soft hazy shaft of sunlight, brighter now among the trees: he smiled and realized that he hadn't heard laughter or felt happiness in a long, long time. He took off his shapeless black hat, held it by the brim, and scaled it upward. He began to laugh too and tears began to run down his cheeks into his matted beard.

Gideon Hassler halted the oxen. He got down slowly, joining the others who had come from behind the wagon, his wife, Oskar and Anna Mittenthaler, Theodosia Grant and her two boys, and Naomi.

Theodosia gasped, then she was running across the needle-cushioned ground toward the men, toward Benedict.

They had entered a grove of trees — scores of them, it seemed — so thick, so towering, so utterly gigantic and beautiful that the eye and the mind could not acknowledge their existence; each one larger than the great lone tree they had found and fled from, that Dallas Mecom had attacked.

Then Benedict had her, swinging her around in a wild dance, then he was crushing her to himself, laughing, kissing her. And she was hugging him, feeling his happiness, laughing and crying with him, knowing the wonder of the earth, of life, of the godlike trees around them.

184